THE LEGO® BATMAN MOVIE

JUNIOR NOVEL

THE LEGO® BATMAN MOVIE

JUNIOR NOVEL

Adapted by
Jeanette Lane
Based on the screenplay by
Seth Grahame-Smith and Chris McKenna & Erik Sommers,
with additional material by
Jared Stern & John Whittington,
based on
LEGO® Construction Toys.

Scholastic Inc.

Published by Scholastic Inc., *Publishers since 1920*. SCHOLASTIC and associated logos are trademarks and/or registered trademarks of Scholastic Inc.

ISBN 978-1-338-11221-4

10 9 8 7 6 5 4 3 2 1   17 18 19 20 21
Printed in the U.S.A.   40
First printing 2017

Book design by Jessica Meltzer

1

High above the busy, buzzing streets of Gotham City, an airplane soared through the clouds. To the aircraft's crew, the troubles of the world below seemed far away. The two pilots, Bill and Dale, were the best of friends.

Pilot Dale picked up his intercom and radioed the air-traffic-control tower. "Gotham Tower, this is McGuffin Airlines Flight 1138. We are transporting eleven million sticks of dynamite, seventeen tons of highly explosive stuff . . ."

"And two best friends!" the pilots chorused.

"We request permission to fly over the most crime-ridden city in the world. Over," Pilot Dale went on.

The air-traffic controllers down below looked at one another.

1

The first air-traffic controller said, "Well, I'm just looking at all the guys' faces here in the control tower, annnnddd . . ."

"I'm good," said the second air-traffic controller.

"Sounds good to me," said the third, nodding.

"Do it!" said the fourth.

"As long as they're best friends," the fifth put in.

"Thumbs-up!" said the sixth.

And so they gave Pilot Dale and Pilot Bill the go-ahead to fly over the heart of Gotham City, where hundreds of thousands of innocent people were going about their daily lives, unaware of the explosive cargo three thousand feet above their heads.

And why should they worry? Gotham City had a secret protector—that is, a protector with a secret identity. It was the one and only Batman!

Batman was a dark, brooding Super Hero who fought the evilest of villains in order to rid the famous city of crime. Although Batman always worked alone, he did have an unwritten agreement with Gotham City's police department. Batman would come if the police flashed the Bat-Signal into the sky. It was a beacon—a sign that there was a renegade defender of justice lurking in the shadows.

Batman had kept his end of the bargain, but he

worked on his terms. He called the shots and defeated the bad guys as he saw fit. He and the longtime police commissioner, Jim Gordon, had an understanding. As long as Commissioner Gordon didn't ask questions, the Caped Crusader would be his right-hand Batman.

"Yep, I think we're cool with that. Have a nice fl—" the first air-traffic controller began. But he broke off suddenly. "Wait a second," he said, leaning toward the radar screen. The radar showed two bright dots—one white and one red—that were far too close to each other. There was more than one vehicle in that flight space.

"McGuffin, do you have a visual of someone on your six?" the second air-traffic controller asked.

A helicopter, black as night, seemed to be approaching the McGuffin craft from the rear. It was hidden by a cluster of clouds.

"Hold on, let me give her a little check-er-ooni," answered Pilot Bill. "I'm looking out the window, and nope, looks like there's nothing following us at all."

In the control room, the two dots were getting closer together. "What do you think?" the first air-traffic controller asked the second.

"If he didn't see anything, I'm sure it's fine," the second air-traffic controller replied.

The first air-traffic controller shrugged and granted the pilots' request. The McGuffin craft headed over central Gotham City.

"Thank you, Gotham Tower," Pilot Dale said. "It's a pleasure flying over you."

But that pleasure was about to come to an abrupt end. The copter dropped from the clouds and landed on top of McGuffin 1138!

A band of Rogues—that is, Gotham City's most dastardly criminals—swarmed from the helicopter onto McGuffin's roof. They were equipped with extra powerful magnetic boots that allowed them to rappel down the side of the plane.

The Rogues prepared to blast open the cargo door. Their mysterious leader announced, "Gentlemen, seal breech in five . . . four . . . three . . . two . . . one . . ."

BOOM! The cargo door flew off its hinges, and the crew of evildoers piled inside the McGuffin's hold.

"What was that?" Pilot Dale wondered from the cockpit.

"One of us should check it out," suggested Pilot Bill.

The two pilots engaged in a friendly battle of Rock, Paper, Scissors.

"Ha! You always do paper!" Pilot Bill crowed.

He'd won, so it was Pilot Dale who had to leave the safety of the cockpit.

The main cabin was empty, but another suspicious noise prompted Pilot Dale to check the cargo hold.

"Yikes!" he exclaimed as a cable of rope wrapped around him. It rolled him up tight and flung him out of the plane. A moment later, his parachute opened, and he began drifting toward the ground.

"Captain Dale, is everything okay?" Pilot Bill asked from the safety of the cockpit.

The mysterious figure who'd dispatched Pilot Dale glanced out of the airplane door and smirked. Pilot Dale's hat had fallen onto the floor of the cargo hold. The figure snatched it up and plopped it on top off his thick, green mop of hair.

"I'm afraid Captain Dale had to bail," he replied. "I'm your new copilot—Captain Joker!"

Uh-oh. Pilot Bill was in real trouble . . . and so was Gotham City. The mysterious leader of this dastardly group was none other than the notorious troublemaker the Joker.

The Joker pulled out his walkie-talkie. "Harley Quinn, are you ready?" he asked his right-hand Rogue.

"I sure am, sugarplum!" Harley replied cheerfully. She revved the engine of her motorcycle.

Down in the streets of Gotham City, a whole gallery of Rogues was ready and waiting right behind her. They were outside the Gotham City Energy Plant, and they were lined up on an impressive array of souped-up vehicles.

The Joker began a Rogue roll call. "Catwoman?" he said.

"Meow, meow!" she replied.

"Penguin?" the Joker asked.

"Rahhhh!" the Penguin growled in response.

"Two-Face?"

"You got it!" Two-Face barked.

"Mr. Freeze?"

"Ice!" Mr. Freeze hissed.

"Poison Ivy?"

"Mwah!" she cried.

"Captain Boomerang?"

"G'day!" he replied.

"Riddler?"

"Riddle me this! What rhymes with Teddy?" the Riddler replied.

The Joker sighed. "Can you just say *yes* or *no*?"

There was a pause.

"Yes," the Riddler said sadly.

"Perfect!" the Joker said. "Gotham City is about to get a load of me!"

2

At Gotham City Police Department, the bad news spread fast.

"Commissioner Gordon! We just got a report that all the B-grade villains are about to break in to the energy plant!" Police Chief O'Hara announced, bursting into the commissioner's office.

A police officer was right on his heels. "And the Joker's headed their way with an absurd amount of explosives!"

"Oh no," replied Commissioner Jim Gordon. "They're working together!"

"What are we going to do, sir?" Chief O'Hara asked.

"The only thing we can do—which, luckily, is

also the only thing we ever do—flip the switch on the Bat-Signal. *Flip!*"

As soon as the commissioner's finger lifted from the Bat-Signal switch, a voice buzzed over his walkie-talkie. "Commissioner, are you there? The Bat-Signal—she's been egged!"

"It's Egghead, sir," Commissioner Gordon said, sighing. "I'm well aware of his work."

After years of helping defend Gotham City's streets from crime, Commissioner Gordon was retiring. He was going to hang up his police cap for good. And he'd expected to take it easy today. He'd thought Batman would take care of whatever trouble the petty criminals attempted.

But the Joker was no petty criminal. He crafted devious, dastardly crimes, and the egg on the Bat-Signal could only mean one thing: The Joker had teamed up with Egghead, a wicked mastermind who could whisk up trouble into a boiling froth.

"All right, let's roll out," said Commissioner Gordon. He and Chief O'Hara rushed through the precinct, making sure their officers were ready. It was going to be a long night.

Meanwhile, more trouble was brewing in front of the Gotham City Energy Plant.

A pizza delivery truck sputtered up to the

plant's locked gate. "I scream, you scream, we all scream for . . . pizza!" sang the truck's jingle.

"All right! I love pizza," Security Guard Sandy said.

"Great," the pizza man insisted. "The toppings are sausage, anchovies, and fear gas!" He opened a pizza box, and a thick fog of gas wafted out. It swirled around Security Guard Sandy until he began to cough.

A vision appeared before Security Guard Sandy's eyes. It was a pizza . . . an enormous, menacing pizza.

"Uhhh . . ." Security Guard Sandy groaned.

"Don't touch the alarm," the scary pizza vision ordered.

You see, this pizza man was no ordinary deliveryman. It was the super-villain known as the Scarecrow! His weapon of choice was a powerful gas that made people see scary things.

As Security Guard Sandy fled from his vision, the Scarecrow drove his pizza truck right into the plant. Harley Quinn and her buddies followed him in.

"Red team, we are inside the perimeter," the Riddler called into his walkie-talkie as he sped by the security checkpoint.

The rest of the corrupt crew was right behind him. They stormed the power plant, driving around the perimeter of the main building. They needed to locate the right entry point.

"Copy that," Clayface replied. "Clayface in position."

"Egghead ready," said Egghead.

"Building breach in fifteen seconds," the Riddler announced.

"We're fifty meters from the door," Captain Boomerang declared.

The Rogues revved their engines, putting pedal to the metal.

"We're thirty meters from the door!" Two-Face bellowed. "Twenty meters! Ten meters! TWO METERS!"

As the Rogues barreled toward the door, security guards scrambled to get out of the way—just in time for Two-Face's monster truck to burst through the door.

The rest of the Rogues drove their trucks straight into the building. One vehicle after another zoomed into the main hallway, throwing the plant workers into a frenzy.

"Get out of the way!" the workers yelled.

"Ahhhh! Run!" yelped another.

"The foxes are in the henhouse!" Two-Face cackled. His truck spun around and slammed its back end into a door. Gas started to seep out into the facility.

"Ahh! Help us! We're under attack!" called a guard as the trucks chased plant workers down a long hallway toward the main core.

The plant's security forces sprang into action, racing through the hallways, trying to track down the Joker's Rogues.

Plant Chief Bill was hurrying toward the control room, taking the emergency stairs. He yelled into his walkie-talkie. "THEY'RE COMING!! Shut everything down. Secure all entrances into this facility!" he commanded.

"On it, Chief!" replied a plant worker, pushing buttons on the complicated control panel.

"Electrify the perimeter fence!" Plant Chief Bill cried, rushing into the control room.

"Yes, sir!" another plant worker replied as he pulled a lever.

"Give me live feeds from all the security cameras!" the chief hollered.

"You bet!" said a third plant worker.

"And Dave and David, shut down the energy core!" the chief ordered.

"Got it, Chief," David's voice came through the walkie-talkie.

Down in the basement, Dave and David stood before a leaky pipe.

"You got that switch, David?" asked Dave.

"I sure do, Dave," David replied. "I'm turning it from on to off." He pulled a massive lever from the ON position to the OFF position.

"Now it's off," said David, sounding pleased with himself.

There was a whirring sound as the plant powered down.

"Deactivating energy core," the energy plant's computer confirmed.

Back in the control room, Plant Chief Bill sighed in relief. "Great job! Now we're almost one hundred percent safe! As long as no one gets past the—"

Before he could finish speaking, a huge ball of clay burst through the control room's doors. It was Clayface!

"RAHHHHH!" he screamed.

The control room's guards aimed their weapons at Clayface. But nothing could slow him down. He charged over to Plant Chief Bill and got right in his face. "Turn on the energy core!"

"Sorry, no one can get in there without Jeff's

12

unique fingerprints, and he's on vacation in Honolulu," Plant Chief Bill replied, shrugging.

At that moment, the doors slid open. Bane and Two-Face strode in, dragging Jeff along with them.

"Aloha, Bill," Jeff said sheepishly.

"Aloha, Jeff," Plant Chief Bill said sadly.

3

Bane popped off Jeff's arm. Another Rogue, Kite Man, glided down and grabbed the arm, bringing it to the special, ultrasecure keypad control screen.

"How kind of Jeff to lend us a *hand*," Kite Man joked, holding the hand up to a keypad.

The pad scanned Jeff's fingerprints, and the plant computer announced, "Reactivating energy core."

The Rogues had all been waiting on their vehicles. The moment the Core Containment Room doors opened, the place was overrun by villains big and small. "Yeah, let's go! Woo-hoo! Yes! Meow, meow," they whooped and hollered.

"Joker, do you read me?" Harley Quinn radioed.

She stood out from the crowd in her black-and-red harlequin getup and famous pigtails. She gazed up at the sky. Above, a plane was approaching.

"Ten-four, girl buddy," came the Joker's voice over the radio.

"We're ready for you, sugarplum!" Harley radioed back.

"Splendid," the Joker answered. "Well then, let's raise the roof!"

With that, Red Hood fired missiles that blazed through the air. They landed on the energy-plant roof with a bang, blasting a huge hole in the facility. The entire city block rattled with the explosion.

"Fire in the hole!" Bane yelled as the building crackled in the charred aftermath.

The explosion put everyone on high alert. Police Commissioner Jim Gordon led the charge as a team of police cars tore down the street.

"Great Caesar's Ghost!" Commissioner Gordon exclaimed. "Chief O'Hara, have you tried the Bat-Phone?"

Of course the chief had tried the Bat-Phone, but he couldn't get through. He was on hold.

In the meantime, the commissioner gave

orders to secure the facility's perimeter. "I want snipers trained on that building," he commanded. "I want water and air support yesterday. And I need SWAT here now!"

Just then, a cop ran up to him. "Phone call for Commissioner Gordon," he said.

The commissioner grabbed the phone. "Hello, Batman?"

"Hi, Jimmy!" a giddy voice replied. "It's the Jokes!"

The commissioner was not at all pleased to hear from him. "Go ahead, Joker!"

"Oh, Commissioner," the Joker responded. "Listen up. At this very minute, a Joker bomb—that's trademarked—is being attached to the inside of the main energy core."

Inside the plant, Batman's old enemy the Penguin, dressed in a stovepipe hat and black-and-white spats, had joined in on the destruction. The Penguin's pet penguins were approaching the energy core, armed with power drills in their slippery little wings. The rest of the Rogues were busy attaching a gigantic Joker bomb to the inside of the main energy core.

"If the mayor isn't here in five minutes to nego-tiate the city's surrender, then we'll blow up the energy core!" the Joker exclaimed.

Inside the Core Containment Room, Croc set the detonator and watched as the timer began to count down. "I did something!" he cheered.

At home, families all around Gotham City were glued to their TVs, watching the heist on the twenty-four-hour news. Nearly every citizen of Gotham City heard the Joker's threats.

"The shock wave will hit Gotham City," the Joker threatened. "And you wouldn't want that, would you? Now give me the mayor! Joker out." He dropped the phone.

"Madam Mayor, I cannot ask you to do this," Commissioner Gordon told Mayor McCaskill, who had rushed to the scene.

"Jim, did you find Batman?" she asked.

"No, ma'am," the commissioner admitted.

"Then we have no choice," she said. "The Joker has the upper hand. We have to surrender Gotham City. I'm sorry."

The mayor climbed in the police helicopter and lifted off. All around the commissioner, SWAT teams took their positions.

The commissioner couldn't believe it had come to this. The bad guys were going to win.

The helicopter flew above the energy plant and hovered there. Slowly, the policemen lowered Mayor McCaskill into the facility. "Lowering mayor package through the hole," the helicopter pilot announced.

When the Rogues saw the mayor, they began driving in tight circles around her. The Scarecrow tried to dive-bomb her from his tiny helicopter. The Riddler revved his lime-green car with jazzy racing stripes. Two-Face lowered and lifted the bucket of his bulldozer.

The Joker strode toward the mayor, a grin plastered on his face. "Madam Mayor, thanks for dropping by."

"I've got only one thing to say to you, Joker," the mayor began, her voice muffled. She was staring at the ground.

"Well, you'd better make it fast," replied the Joker, pointing to his watch as a handy reminder for the mayor that nearby, there was a bomb with a timer on it.

"Do you ever play roulette?" the mayor asked in a low voice.

"On occasion" was the Joker's response.

"Well, let me give you a word of advice," said the mayor.

"I'm all ears," replied the Joker.

"When playing roulette . . ."

The mayor paused. When she looked up at the Joker, he realized something.

Batman was on the scene! Somehow, he had snuck in behind the mayor.

Batman stepped out from behind the mayor and leaped high in the air.

"Always bet on BLACK!" he declared.

4

BATMAN?!?" the Joker cried. "What are you doing? You're completely outnumbered here. Are you nuts?"

"You wanna get nuts?" Batman yelled. "Come on. Let's get nuts!"

"Get him!" the Joker cried to his henchmen.

The Joker's many Rogues and henchmen descended on Batman. With a *POW* and a *SMASH* and a *SLAM*, Batman battled them all. He whirlwind-kicked and power-punched and karate-kicked and counterpunched. He threw a few Batarangs and took out twenty bad guys in one fell swoop.

Two-Face fired rounds at Batman from his souped-up bulldozer, but Batman battled back with Batarangs. "In your Face-es," Batman cried.

The Riddler aimed his car right at Batman, calling, "Riddle me this, Batman! When is—"

Batman didn't wait to hear the rest of the riddle. He snatched Harley Quinn's mallet and threw it at the Riddler's vehicle. The long handle of the mallet landed in a tire, flipping the car in the air.

"*Punch* line," quipped Batman.

"Don't attack him one at a time," the Joker hollered. The Rogues needed a different strategy if they had any chance of defeating Batman.

"Computer," Batman called into the comm link on his wrist. "Overcompensate!"

"I'm on my way, sir," Computer responded.

Within seconds, the Batmobile exploded through a wall.

"Kaboom," said Computer.

"Yeah!" cheered Batman. "Computer! Where's the bomb?"

After a quick scan of the facility, Computer said, "The bomb is located at the base of the energy core."

"Come on, guys, fight dirty!" the Joker half demanded, half begged. He had worked too hard on this plan for it to fail already. "Clayface, literally throw dirt in his eyes!"

Clayface did just that, briefly blinding Batman,

but the Caped Crusader still fought with precision and might.

A full-on blast from Clayface landed Batman on his knees. When he looked up, he was face-to-face with a horde of penguins. They were eyeing him with their little round, yellow eyes.

"Penguins," Batman muttered. "My least favorite movie animal." Batman tried to shoo the birds away. Then he leaped into the Batmobile, which quickly converted into a jet known as Black Thunder. It rose into the air and sped toward the main building of the energy plant.

Mr. Freeze shot ice rays at the aircraft, and Black Thunder plummeted to the ground. It skidded into a large hangar.

Batman threw a Batarang to the power plant's ceiling, but Poison Ivy was already in position. As soon as he landed on the catwalk, Poison Ivy had him tangled in her vines.

"Kiss me, Batman!" Poison Ivy taunted him.

Batman knew just one smooch from the toxic villain could mean certain death! He quickly grabbed a penguin and used it as a shield.

Batman felt a cool draft. He glanced over his shoulder. It was Mr. Freeze! Again!

There were too many Rogues and only one

Batman—and one very big bomb. "Computer, I need a little firepower!" Batman called out.

A large, fiery vehicle burst into the energy core room and scorched Mr. Freeze with its flaming jets. Next, it cut the thorny ties of Poison Ivy's vines.

Batman leaped from the catwalk and landed on the main floor with his cape fluttering behind him. He wasn't surprised to find a ton of new bad guys waiting for him. Batman knocked out all of them, but he still hadn't gotten closer to the Joker bomb.

"How is he beating all of you AGAIN?" the Joker wondered.

The Caped Crusader had an answer: "'Cuz I'm Batmaaaaaaaaaaan!"

"Everybody run!" cried Harley Quinn.

The Joker had heard enough. He wrapped his fingers around the steering wheel of his car and headed straight for Batman.

Batman grabbed onto the hood of the speeding car and held on for dear life.

"Hi, Batman," the Joker yelled into a bullhorn. "So weird to keep *running into* you!" He giggled as he aimed his car for a concrete wall.

WHACK! The Joker bailed out of the vehicle

as it burst into flames. Meanwhile, Batman had gracefully leaped out of the car's way.

"Looks like your plan failed," Batman said.

"Well, it's only a matter of time before I take over Gotham City," the Joker claimed as he pulled out his weapon.

Batman took cover behind a pile of rubble. "When has that ever happened?" he asked the Joker. He spoke into his comm link. "Computer?"

"Calculating . . . never," answered Computer.

Popping up from behind the rubble heap, Batman threw a Batarang and tripped the Joker. "You know why?" Batman prompted, feeling smug. "Because I'm always one step ahead of you."

. The Joker threw a mini bomb that exploded with a *bang*. "And I always get away!" There was a cloud of fumes, and the Joker's voice seemed to fade.

When the smoke lifted, the Joker was floating away on a balloon.

"Not this time," Batman grumbled. He rushed forward and leaped up to grab the Joker's hand. "Because this time, I got you—"

"Oh yeah?" The Joker sounded amused. "Well, there's only one problem: Who's gonna defuse the bomb?"

Batman hung on to the Joker as the balloon

rose higher and drifted over the plant's energy core. At last, Batman spied the bomb. With curly wires and a big red ticker, it was much larger than the one the Joker had used moments before. It was certain to set off a chain reaction. If it ignited, it could blow the whole plant sky-high.

The bomb ticked down. Only seconds remained.

"It's gotta be one or the other, Batman," the Joker pointed out triumphantly. "Save the city or catch your greatest enemy." He grinned. "You can't do both."

"I'm sorry, what did you just say?" Batman asked.

"I said, 'You can't do both,'" repeated the Joker.

"No, I mean the other thing."

"Save the city or catch your greatest enemy?" the Joker tried again.

"Enemy," Batman said the word slowly, thoughtfully.

"Yeah."

"You think you're my greatest enemy?" Batman asked the Joker, his voice drenched with disbelief.

"YES! Who else do you have an intense, cool, psychological relationship with?" the Joker demanded.

"Bane," replied Batman without much thought. Batman liked to battle with Bane.

"No, you don't," replied the Joker, sounding insulted.

"Superman," offered Batman.

"Superman's not a bad guy," the Joker protested.

"If it's not Superman, then I'd say that I don't currently have *a* bad guy," Batman concluded. "I am fighting a few different people."

"What?" the Joker asked incredulously.

"I like to spread the pain around," Batman explained, shrugging.

"Okay, look," the Joker continued. "I'm fine with you fighting other people if you want to do that, but what we have? This is special. So when people ask you who's your number-one bad guy, you say . . ."

"Superman."

"Are you seriously saying that there is noth-ing—NOTHING—special about us?"

"Let me tell you something, J-Bird," Batman began, "there is no 'us.' Never has been; never will be. You're a clown who means nothing to me."

Despite the smile smeared across his face, the Joker looked like he was in pain.

"Now if you'll excuse me," Batman said, glancing at the intense drop to the ground, "I've got to defuse that bomb."

Batman let go of the Joker, and the green-haired bad guy floated sadly away.

5

Batman plunged down to the energy plant and got to work deactivating the bomb. It was no sweat.

"Batman! You did it!" Commissioner Gordon cheered.

"Yeah, you did it, Batman!" the relieved people in the street cheered.

"Yeah, I did it again!" Batman agreed, not surprised in the least.

"Whoa, that was stressful," said Commissioner Gordon. "It's a good thing I'm retiring."

"Don't remind me, J-Dog," said Batman. "You're making me so emotional."

"Thank you, Batman," yelled a grateful fan.

"My pleasure," answered Batman, his voice especially deep and gravelly.

"We love you!" another citizen called out.

"Thank you! I'm blushing so hard under the mask," he responded.

It felt like just another day to Batman, another crisis overcome. The city was always thanking him for his heroics. After all, he was Batman.

"*Grazie*, Batman!" a citizen called.

"*Prego*," Batman replied, nodding.

"Hey, Batman, can I have a photo?" another citizen asked.

"Of course," said Batman. He leaned in for the picture.

"Thank you!" the citizen said.

"Five dollars a photo," said Batman. He waited as the citizen counted out his money.

"You're the best, Batman!" cried a fan.

"Oh, I'm humble," Batman said.

"Thanks, Batman!" said another fan.

"I'm totally modest about it. Thank you," said Batman, puffing up his chest.

At last, Batman gave a grand wave and strode over to the Batmobile. He drove away slowly, allowing his fans extra time to take in the sight of him— his cheeky grin, his cape flowing in the wind, his features accented by the black-and-charcoal interior of the Batmobile.

Batman drove through the city's busy center

square, and people hung out of the windows, yelling and waving. Everyone was thrilled to see the city's hero.

As Batman waved and acknowledged his fans, he was overcome by a funny feeling. He took a deep breath. "Computer!" he called to the fancy dashboard of the Batmobile.

"Go ahead," Computer responded.

"Are we near the orphanage?" asked Batman.

"Yes."

"Great! Let's turn those frowns upside down," Batman said enthusiastically.

Batman slowed down as he approached a massive building with a large green lawn. The yard was filled with children.

When Batman honked, all the orphans stopped what they were doing.

"That sounds like the Batmobile!" cried a boy with glasses. His name was Dick Grayson, and he was sitting on top of the orphanage's sign. From his perch, he could identify the Batmobile and— even better—its driver. "No way! Hey, orphans. Look who's here!" he cried.

Dick was nimble and quick. He expertly leaped from the sign and sprang toward the Batmobile. But he was instantly trampled by

the mob of orphans running toward the hero's car.

Before Dick had a chance to straighten his glasses, the other kids had all flocked to the area by the fence.

"Oh my gosh, it's Batman!" one kid yelled.

"Hooray!" cheered the whole crew.

"Hey, kids," Batman called out. "Who wants a shot from the merch gun?"

Batman pulled out what looked like a toy bazooka and aimed it at the crowd.

"I do! I do!" the kids replied, jumping up and down.

"Great!" Batman shot the gun, and it launched an impressive variety of Batman gear over the orphanage fence. The kids scrambled to snatch up the prizes.

"The rest of you get Bat Bucks! Redeemable online," Batman announced. He shot the merch gun again, and coupons fluttered in the sky in a flurry of fake money.

The orphans chanted Batman's name with glee—all except Dick Grayson. The kid who'd been first to recognize Batman was the only one left empty-handed. He watched longingly as the Batmobile revved away.

Meanwhile, Batman was patting himself on the back. He had given a bunch of orphans all kinds of swag. He'd made them happy. This made Batman feel especially heroic.

As the Batmobile neared Wayne Island, Computer asked for the password.

A password? Wayne Island? What was going down?

Well, in case you didn't know, Wayne Island is named for one of Gotham City's greatest families. The only living member of that family was the ace businessman Bruce Wayne. Because he was rich and handsome and gave money to good causes, a lot of people respected Bruce Wayne. He had a very busy social calendar, and he was known to be the life of every party he attended.

Bruce had become an orphan at a young age. Ever since that time, Alfred, the Wayne family's wise and kind butler, had looked after him. Even though Bruce was now a grown man, Alfred still looked after him. They lived together in Wayne Manor, on Wayne Island.

The reason any of this is important is that the Batcave was also on Wayne Island. It was located directly beneath Wayne Manor. This

was convenient because Bruce Wayne was also Batman, and Batman was also Bruce Wayne.

When someone lives in extreme luxury on the edge of a crime-ridden city, security is very important. Therefore, the island required a password.

Batman recited the password with a smug smile. "BATMAN RULES."

"Thank you," Computer responded, and the doors to the secret, hidden entrance of the secret, hidden Batcave slid open.

6

Batman parked the Batmobile in the Batcave. Then he thought ahead to his plans for the evening. He had to pay his electric bill. Geez, Computer used a lot of juice.

Batman aimed the remote at his gigantic TV screen. The news turned on. "It must be a great time to be Batman," Anchorman Phil declared. "I can only imagine he's going home right now to party the night away surrounded by tons of friends."

Batman frowned. "Hey, Computer! I'm home!"

His words echoed through the luxurious but empty Batcave.

Computer cued up some music with a phat beat as Batman got his evening started.

"Hey, Computer, put this bomb in the museum," Batman said, holding up the bomb he'd defused earlier.

"Certainly, sir," Computer replied. A robotic arm reached out, grabbed the bomb, and placed it carefully next to another huge explosive.

"Thank you," said Batman.

"No worries," Computer replied.

"Anything exciting happen while I was gone?" Batman asked.

"You have four pieces of mail," Computer said.

"Great," said Batman. "What did I get?"

"You have this week's penny saver, two bills, and a coupon for the local supermarket," Computer said. "It expires in two weeks, but I've heard that some stores will honor it past the expiration date."

"Copy that," said Batman.

"Also, Alfred is on the seventeenth floor, grouting tiles in the second bathroom of the fifth master bedroom," Computer informed him.

Batman looked disappointed. "How long does that take?"

"The estimated drying time is twenty-four hours, but it's recommended to wait ten days before exposing the surface to moisture."

Batman sighed. It was a lot of work, keeping track of a manor and a Batcave. He aimed a grappling hook at a moving platform and used it to pull himself up to his movable closet to change into something more comfortable.

The closet was filled with Batman outfits for every occasion: Thanksgiving Chic; Fourth of July Patriot; Aquatic Explorer. Batman took off that day's suit and put on a simple, knee-length robe. But he kept on his cowl—that is, his Batman mask.

"Thanks for the update," Batman said. "Have Alfred move me out of there. And I should probably have something for dinner."

"Alfred left Lobster Thermidor in the fridge."

"Oh, that's my favorite," Batman said. "I can't wait." He took the elevator down to the kitchen. Then he put the dish in the microwave and pushed 20:00.

"Oh, not twenty minutes, silly," he muttered to himself. He reset the clock to 2:00. Then he gazed longingly at the Lobster Thermidor as it slowly spun inside the microwave.

When the creamy concoction was finally warm, he took it to the Batboat. Surrounded by lots of aquatic Bat-vehicles, he slid into the boat's driver's seat and ate his solitary meal.

When he was done, Batman stretched. Then he pulled out his electric guitar. It was time to rock out with some post-Thermidor jams.

Batman glanced at his watch. It was still early. He went to the manor's theater to watch a movie. Next, he played in the manor's pool with his finned friend, Dolphy.

At last, it was time to brush his teeth. On his way to bed, he stopped to look at the family photos hanging in Wayne Manor's parlor.

"Hey, Mom, Hey, Dad. I, uh, saved the city again today," he whispered. His gaze lingered on the photo. "I think you would've been really proud."

"There you are—" a nearby voice said. It was Alfred, who had known Batman back when he was just Bruce Wayne.

Batman was startled. "Hi-yah!" he cried, kicking Alfred into his grand piano. The lid crashed down on top of the butler's head.

Alfred slowly lifted the lid and emerged, rubbing the back of his head.

"Alfred! I am so sorry," Batman said. "I have incredible reflexes."

"No, no," said Alfred, stepping gingerly out of the piano. "It's my fault. I should've known better than to sneak up on you like that."

"Sorry," Batman said again. "I was just lost in

thought, and as you know, when I'm in there, I'm in deep."

"Were you looking at the family pictures again?"

"At the what?" Batman asked, trying to cover his embarrassment. He lifted his stare from the floor to the wall of photographs in front of him. "At the old family . . . oh yes. I see what you mean. Look at that. The old gang."

It was a full-on gallery. There were photos taken at exotic locations on expensive vacations with palm trees, turquoise waters, marble fountains. There were photos on horseback and skydiving. There were photos of the family in front of Wayne Manor, dwarfed by its massive size. But Batman's gaze did not linger on any of these. He couldn't take his eyes off a close-up photograph of his younger self with his parents: father, mother, and son. They were smiling, happy to be together. Alfred had taken that one.

"Yeah," Batman said. "Uh, no, I wasn't."

"I see," said Alfred, his deep voice full of understanding. "Sir, if you don't mind my saying, I'm a little concerned. I've seen you have similar phases in the past. Do you want to talk about what you're feeling right now?"

Batman scowled. "I don't talk about feelings, Alfred. I don't have any. I've never seen one. I'm

a night-stalking, crime-fighting vigilante and a heavy-metal rapping machine. I don't feel anything emotionally except for rage. 24/7, 365 days a year, at a million percent. And if you think that there's something behind that, then you're crazy. Good night, Alfred."

Alfred was not crazy. The devoted butler knew that Bruce Wayne's sorrow from the loss of his parents had driven him to become Batman. He knew that Bruce had not had a day of peace since his parents had died.

Alfred was worried about Bruce. He was worried that Bruce might be the crazy one, because Bruce had just said "good night," even though the sun was rising above the towers at the top of Wayne Manor.

"But, sir, it's morning," Alfred pointed out. He opened the heavy drapes that covered the parlor's panoramic windows.

"Master Bruce, you live on an island, figuratively and literally," Alfred said.

"Yeah, I love it."

Alfred sighed. "You can't spend the rest of your life alone, dressed in black, listening to angry music, and staying up all night," he insisted.

"Yes, I can. 'Cuz I'm Batman."

"But don't you think it's time you finally faced . . . your greatest fear?" Alfred asked.

"Snakes?" suggested Batman.

"No."

"Clowns?" Batman guessed again.

"No."

"Snake clowns?" Batman asked with a shudder.

"Bruce, listen," Alfred said seriously. "Your greatest fear is . . . being part of a family again."

Bruce/Batman considered what Alfred had said. He looked at the family picture on the wall. The pain was almost too much for him to take.

"Nope," Batman said. "My greatest fear is snake clowns because you put that idea in my head."

"Sir, this is my fault," Alfred said sadly. "I should've done a better job raising you."

Desperate for a distraction, Batman began his exercise routine. "Time for push-ups! One . . . two . . . we're going to a thousand! Three . . . four . . ."

"I'm afraid that's not possible, sir," said Alfred.

"It *is* possible," insisted Batman. "I'm already at twenty."

"You're scheduled to go to Jim Gordon's retirement party," his butler replied, changing the subject.

"What, no! I don't wanna do that." Bruce pouted, his lower lip sticking way out.

"You're going to have a great time," Alfred said coaxingly.

"No, no, no!" Bruce cried.

"Jim Gordon will really appreciate it." Alfred continued with his reasonable line of thinking.

"No, no, no!" Bruce continued with his unreasonable refusal.

"You'll get to meet the new commissioner," Alfred pointed out, his voice bright.

"No, no, no, no, no, no, no!" Bruce exploded into a full-on temper tantrum that would have been impressive even for a three-year-old. He kicked and screamed and pounded the ground with his full-grown fists. He even rolled up and down the stairs. The parlor walls trembled.

Alfred shook his head. He had hoped it wouldn't come to this, but he was going to have to do it.

"And before you go, we can do your favorite thing," he suggested calmly.

Gasp! Sniff, sniff. Bruce looked up at Alfred with tear-stained eyes.

"Tuxedo dress-up party?!" he asked hopefully.

When Alfred nodded, Bruce sat up eagerly.

He would go to the party like a big boy.

7

As Alfred drove Bruce Wayne's limousine to the commissioner's going-away party, he glanced in the rearview mirror. "Sir, are you forgetting something?"

"Nope," Batman replied from the backseat. He was dressed in his favorite tuxedo, and he was preening a little in the mirror.

"Your cowl, sir?" Alfred prompted.

"My what now?" Batman replied.

"Your . . . armored face disguise, sir," he said. "It's still on."

"Aw, come on," said Bruce. "Can't I just go as Batman?"

"But everyone is expecting to see Bruce Wayne," Alfred reminded him.

"Nobody wants to see Bruce Wayne!" Batman

protested. "Here are his likes: crying like a baby, talking about feelings, being a dumb robot, and doing boring stuff. Batman, on the other hand, is a crime fighter with the heart of a tiger and the skin of a bat!"

Alfred shot Batman his sternest look. "Bruce . . ."

"Fine," Batman replied, pulling off his mask.

Bruce Wayne looked tired and sad. He didn't look like the suave, superstar businessman who was on the cover of all those magazines. In the backseat of the limo, he looked human.

"Happy now?" Bruce asked Alfred.

"Indubitably."

"Good," Bruce responded. "Must be nice to be happy." Then he turned his attention to the news. It was handy to have a TV built into the limo.

But when he realized the reporter was doing a feature on a different Super Hero, Superman, Bruce quickly looked away.

All the way across town, the Joker was watching the same television station. He rolled his eyes when he saw Superman on the screen. As if it wasn't bad enough that Batman would not acknowledge the depth of their relationship, now the news had to fuss over the Super Hero Batman claimed was his greatest enemy.

"They're really more like rivals," the Joker mumbled to himself. Still, he paid attention to the interview.

Reporter Pipa Expositionay was standing next to a very tall man with a very square jaw and wavy dark hair. "Tonight, on *Metropolis Corner*, we have our favorite star—Superman."

"Hi, Gotham City," chirped Superman with a hearty wave.

"Superman," Pipa began, "tell me how you feel about the recent banishment of your archenemy to the Phantom Zone."

Superman rubbed his chin and leaned in to the microphone. "Well, it's complicated, Pipa. When you're Superman, you battle a lot of villains, but none of them are as special as *my* super-villain."

"See?" the Joker exclaimed. "Superman gets it! Why can't Batman?"

He couldn't believe how clearly Superman had just illustrated his point, but no one else seemed to care. The Rogues weren't even paying attention. They were in the other room, playing cards and goofing off.

Behind the Joker, Bane had just built a CD rack out of toothpicks. "Check it out, guys! I built a CD rack!" he cried proudly.

A moment later, the rack fell apart . . . and Bane strained his back bending over to pick up the pieces. "My back," he groaned.

The Joker sighed. "How am I supposed to get Batman's respect when I'm working with these losers?" he wondered despairingly.

"You know, Mr. J, sometimes the best way to get something you really, really want is to act like you don't want it at all," said Harley Quinn. She knew what she was talking about. She had a degree in psychiatry.

Meanwhile, Superman's interview continued. "Yeah, Pipa," Superman explained. "I couldn't put him in just a regular prison. He had to go somewhere special—the Phantom Zone."

"The Phantom Zone, of course, is a notorious space jail that houses every hero's biggest villain," Pipa Expositionay explained.

"You know it," agreed Superman. "They've got all the sickest baddies up there."

Sitting in his hideout, the Joker was hatching a new plan. "Hmmm, I'm starting to get an idea," he said thoughtfully.

A moment later, he bolted upright. "Gentlemen and ladies, I'm going to show Batman that it's not over between us. In fact, we've only just begun!"

The Joker rubbed his hands together. He couldn't wait to start on his new scheme.

When the limo pulled up to the party, Bruce Wayne plastered a dashing smile onto his face. It was showtime, whether he liked it or not.

The flashes from the cameras were blinding. Reporters were everywhere, yelling questions about his clothes and his recent dates. Bruce wished he were at home eating Lobster Thermidor. Computer never asked him such idiotic questions.

Bruce braced himself. "Okay, shutterbugs, look alive," he declared, pointing at the various cameras. "I'm going to give you three poses. Ready? Kissy face." He pursed his lips for five seconds. "Oops, I did it again." He made a shocked expression for the count of five. "And the Bad Boy. Whatcha gonna do?" His last pose looked pretty normal, except he squinted his eyes. "I'm out of here, guys. Thank you."

Bruce strode into the party, greeting various attendees along the way.

"Bruce, any advice for the new commissioner?" a partygoer asked him.

"As long as he can turn on the Bat-Signal, he'll be fine," Bruce answered with a smirk. After all, no one—except Alfred—knew that he was secretly Batman. But everyone knew that Batman had been Commissioner Jim Gordon's best ally in defeating crime on the streets of Gotham City.

The gala event was filled with people who admired Bruce Wayne, and Bruce did his best to be the cool, clever, macho man that the people of Gotham City expected him to be.

"Bruce," said one of the state's senators, approaching him. "I don't know how you did it."

"You can't prove it, you didn't do it," Bruce replied with a charming smile.

"Mr. Wayne, so great to see you! Come join us!" said the prime minister of a very important country, who just happened to be standing nearby.

With all the excitement, Bruce didn't even notice that there was a choir there singing. He certainly didn't realize that the choir was an orphan choir. And he especially didn't realize that the kid who had been sitting on the sign in the orphanage yard—the one who had been the most excited to spot Batman—was one of the orphans in the choir. That kid, Dick Grayson, spotted Bruce Wayne right away.

"No way!" Dick said. "It's Bruce Wayne! He's the greatest orphan of all time!"

As soon as the song was over, Dick ran toward Bruce. "Mr. Wayne!" he called out, weaving his way through the crowd.

Bruce nodded at the eager kid. "You want a picture?" he asked in his cheery celebrity voice.

"That would be swell," replied Dick.

"Here we go," he announced, whipping out a phone and taking a selfie—of just himself. He flashed Dick a smile. "Party face. Boom! Keep it," he said, tossing Dick the phone.

"Whoa! Thanks, Mr. Wayne," Dick said, clutching the phone to his chest.

"Call me Bruce, champ."

"I'm just so jazzed to meet you, sir," said Dick.

"I'm sorry, did you say 'jazzed'?" Bruce asked incredulously.

"Yes! My name's Richard Grayson," the orphan introduced himself, "but all the kids at the orphanage call me Dick."

He waited patiently as a stream of gala attendants approached Bruce Wayne, wanting to meet him.

"So, I had a question for you, sir," Dick said when he got the chance.

"Okay, hit me with it," Bruce Wayne replied, but he wasn't really paying attention to Dick. He was waving at a member of the Gotham City Council across the room.

"As the most successful orphan ever—"

"Thank you, I appreciate it."

"Do you have any advice on how to get adopted?" Dick asked.

"Oh yeah," Bruce replied again, but he still wasn't really paying attention.

"You do?"

Bruce was distracted by someone asking for an autograph, so Dick tried a different approach. "Okay, for example, is teeth whitener a good idea?"

"Yes, here you go, pal," Bruce said, handing over an autograph to a charming woman with silver hair.

"Really?"

"Oh yeah."

"Looking good, Bruce," someone called from the crowd.

"How about eyeliner or a Cajun accent?" Dick asked.

"Try both," answered Bruce.

"Look! It's the new commissioner!" someone yelled. At that moment, there was a huge commotion. There was a young woman at the center of a crowd. She was standing right next to Jim Gordon, the retiring police commissioner. Bruce wanted to know who she was.

"Mr. Wayne? Should I get experimental surgery to make my eyes larger and more vulnerable looking?" Dick asked, even though it was clear that Bruce was no longer paying attention.

"Do that," Bruce mumbled.

"Wow. Fascinating. Um, Mr. Wayne, are you currently in the market to adopt a child?" Dick asked hopefully.

"Yeah," Bruce Wayne responded without thinking. All his thoughts were on the woman walking in with Commissioner Gordon.

"Really?" Dick prompted.

"Oh yeah," Bruce said, but he had no idea what he was saying.

"Are you looking for more of a base-model orphan, or one that has upgraded features, like talent in cooking or driftwood art?" Dick kept going.

"Yep," was Bruce's response.

"Deep-sea welding?"

"Yeah."

"How about an orphan who can do street magic?"

"All of it sounds great."

"Really?" Dick tried to confirm. "Because all of it sounds like me. Mr. Wayne, do you think you'd be interested in adopting me as your future orphan son?"

"Definitely."

"You mean that, Mr. Wayne?"

"A million percent." But a million percent of Bruce Wayne's attention was on Commissioner Jim Gordon and the woman he was escorting, or who was escorting him.

"This is great!" Dick yelled, doing a fist pump. "Because all I want is to get adopted so I can finally stop being . . ."

Dick looked up and realized that Bruce Wayne was gone.

". . . alone."

8

It was the big moment at the gala. Everyone's attention was on the stage at the far end of the elegant ballroom. There was a podium and an oversize screen behind it. The mayor was speaking into the microphone. "We've gathered here tonight to mark the retirement of Jim Gordon," she announced, patting the commissioner on the shoulder.

"Good-bye!" former Commissioner Gordon said to the crowd, leaning in to the microphone.

"And wish him well in his South African safari expedition," the mayor added with a smile.

"Thank you," Commissioner Gordon added.

"And now, to introduce you to his exciting, new replacement," the mayor said, motioning to the gigantic screen behind her. "Everyone, meet your

new commissioner. Enjoy this special video we prepared for you!"

The screen lit up behind the mayor, and fireworks exploded around the face of a young woman—the same young woman who had walked into the gala with the former commissioner, Jim Gordon.

"Meet Barbara Gordon! The new commissioner of Gotham City! She was top of her class at Harvard for Police," a booming voice narrated. The video continued to show the new commissioner, Barbara Gordon, in many impressive situations: shining in her police classes, heading up SWAT team strikes, working with other top police people to get things done.

The video shared many highlights of Barbara Gordon's early career. "We're going to take down these perps together," the on-screen Barbara Gordon declared.

"Meet Barbara Gordon, the new commissioner of Gotham City!" the video narrator concluded.

The audience clapped loudly as Barbara Gordon approached the stage.

"Congratulations, darling," her dad said, smiling at her proudly.

"Thanks, Dad," said Barbara.

"Here she is, everyone," said the mayor.

Barbara strode across the stage and up to the podium. "Thank you! Thanks!" Barbara said into the microphone. "Dad, you've always done a great job protecting Gotham City."

"Flip!" said her dad, flipping the Bat-Signal switch.

"Along with Batman, of course," Barbara said.

From the audience, Bruce Wayne applauded wildly. "Woo! Let's hear it for Batman!"

"Who I wish were here right now," Barbara went on.

"Oh, I'm sure he's listening ... heh heh," said Bruce, winking.

"Because if he were, I think Batman would agree that Gotham City would never just accept the status quo."

"Oh, we hate the status quo," Bruce agreed.

"Yeah, we're sick of it!" agreed another gala attendee.

Barbara took a deep breath. "I'd like to ask all of you a question: Are you fed up with crime?"

The audience's answer was clear: Yes. They were all fed up with crime.

"We're all tired of crime," Bruce agreed. "You bet."

"Are you fed up with the endless stream of villains causing havoc on our streets?" Barbara questioned.

The audience was fed up with the villains! They all agreed, as did Bruce Wayne.

"That shouldn't even be a question," he answered.

"Great," the new commissioner continued. "Then let's talk about real improvements that will end the cycle of crime."

"You literally have me eating out of the palm of your curved hand," Bruce murmured.

The audience was on board, too. They listened closely. This new commissioner had a lot to say!

"I've got a four-point pilot program that I'd love to share with you," said Barbara Gordon.

"I want to hear all four points," Bruce admitted.

"It's called . . . ," Barbara set up her plan, "it takes a village . . ."

"Great start . . . I am ready," Batman said, quietly cheering her on.

". . . not a Batman," Barbara finished.

"Terrible ending," Bruce grumbled, annoyed by this sudden turn in events.

"Look, Batman's been on the job for a very, very, very, very, very, very long time," Barbara tried to explain. "However, in spite of having a full-time Batman, Gotham City is still the most crime-ridden city in the *world*."

The audience—unlike Bruce Wayne—was still in total agreement with the new commissioner. They mumbled about how she was right and how, historically speaking, it was true that Batman had not been entirely effective.

"He hasn't captured the Riddler. He hasn't captured Bane. Or Catwoman, or Two-Face, or *any* of Gotham City's other villains," Barbara went on.

"You know, she's right!" an audience member murmured.

"Huh," said another.

"She's making a lot of sense," said a third. "Batman's not good at his job . . ."

"And that includes the Joker," Barbara said.

"We love you, Barbara!" the audience cried.

Bruce Wayne couldn't take it anymore. "Um, hi there. Excuse me? I'm so sorry," he said as he made his way through the crowd. "Excuse me," he asserted as he climbed up to the stage and approached the podium. "Ahem. Ahem. AHEM."

"Yes?" Barbara prompted.

"Hi. Bruce Wayne," he said, standing up ridiculously straight. "Billionaire, bon vivant, Gotham City's most eligible bachelor, like, ninety years in a row."

"I know who you are, Mr. Wayne," the new commissioner assured him.

"You bet you do. Quick questch," Bruce said, shortening the word *question* for no apparent reason. "What's your problem with Batman?" He glared at Barbara Gordon with his intense, brooding eyes.

"I'm glad you asked, Mr. Wayne. I'm not a Batman hater," Barbara Gordon explained, "but we don't need an unsupervised, adult man in a Halloween costume karate chopping poor people. We need to take what's good about Batman and marry it to actual laws and proper ethics and accountability."

"I hate everything you just said," Bruce growled.

"Because my dream is for the police force . . . ," Barbara began, ignoring Bruce and looking out at the audience, "*to team up* with Batman."

"No!" Bruce yelled.

"Yeah, wouldn't that be better?" Barbara asked. She clicked a button, and a picture of her and Batman appeared on the screen. Its caption read BARBARA AND BATMAN WORKING SIDE BY SIDE. The picture had obviously been doctored.

"No!" Bruce insisted. "Those are all things I hate."

"And I know that, together, the World's Greatest Detective and Gotham City's Finest could clean up these crime-ridden streets . . . forever!"

The crowd stared at Barbara, dumbfounded.

"Because, as I always say—" Barbara began, but she stopped abruptly. A large number of ice-cream trucks were surrounding the gala.

Bruce had noticed the trucks, too. Something about those ice-cream trucks was very, very wrong.

Pizza, pizza, let's have a pizza ice cream . . . sang the truck jingle.

"EVERYBODY GET DOWN!" Barbara and Bruce yelled at the same time.

Heavily armed clowns began pouring out of the trucks.

BOOM! An explosion ripped a hole in the wall.

A moment later, the Joker emerged through the smoke. "Grand entrance!"

The gala turned into absolute chaos as the Joker's Rogues invaded.

"Everyone, make your way to the exits immediately," Barbara ordered the audience.

"Ahhh!" screamed various audience members.

"I don't know where the exits are!" screamed others.

Croc hurried to the main exit. "I'm blocking!" he crowed.

"Rogues Two, bring me the mayor!" the Joker barked into his walkie-talkie.

"We're on it," came a staticky growl in reply.

"Ten-four!" cried Kite Man.

"And, Harley Quinn, you know what to do," the Joker went on.

"I sure do, sugarplum," she responded and dashed off, away from the crowd.

Meanwhile, Bruce Wayne had forced his way through the crowd and over to the emergency exit. He raced up the fire escape, checking his PROXIMITY INDICATOR WATCH as he took the stairs two at a time. "Butler One!" he said into his comm link. "This is Bat One! Do you copy?"

"Go ahead, Bat One," came Alfred's voice from the high-tech watch. The good butler was still in the limo, parked just outside the gala. He was busy reading a pamphlet titled "Setting Limits on Your Out-of-Control Child."

"I need my cowl, NOW!" Bruce cried.

"Only if you say the magic word," Alfred replied calmly.

Bruce gritted his teeth. "Alfred, I don't have time for magic words."

Alfred sighed. "Okay, sir. We'll talk about that back at the Batcave." He punched a button on the limo's console.

Bruce leaped off the roof just in time for his cowl to fall over his head. Instantly, he was suiting up, transforming into Batman. He threw out a grappling hook.

"Computer, initialize MasterBuild music!" he

called. "I need to take out multiple targets with minimal damage. Hopefully."

"May I suggest the Scuttler, sir?" Computer replied.

"Perfect," said Batman. He began Master-Building one of his favorite vehicles.

Meanwhile, back inside the gala, Barbara was determined to protect the mayor from the Joker and his Rogues.

"Madam Mayor, stay close to me," she said, pulling the mayor to safety behind the podium.

Mr. Freeze and Clayface aimed their weapons at Mayor McCaskill and the new commissioner.

"We're pinned down!" Barbara called into her walkie-talkie. She turned to the mayor. "On my signal, head for the south exit."

She and the mayor stood up and started racing through the crowd. Rogues attacked them as they hurried along, but Barbara was undeterred. She threw punches and kicks, jabbing with her elbows and even using some of Clayface's mud to blind her opponents.

Slowly but surely, Barbara made her way to the Joker. "Chief O'Hara, extraction protocol," she said into her walkie. "We're coming in hot!"

She and the mayor made their way through a small flock of penguins, finally reaching an exit.

Barbara kicked the door down. Chief O'Hara was waiting on the other side with backup.

"Chief, get the mayor to safety," Barbara panted.

"Yes, ma'am," replied the chief.

Now that the mayor was safe, Barbara turned her attention back to the Joker. She narrowed her eyes. "Team, I've got the Joker in my sights," she said into her walkie-talkie. She began striding toward the Joker, who was too busy enjoying the mayhem he'd created to notice her approach.

But just before Barbara reached him—

"OH YEAHHHHH!" cried Batman, bursting through the wall in the Scuttler. It was an awesome machine with legs instead of wheels—good for climbing stairs, walls, and ceilings—and all kinds of other features.

The Scuttler landed right in between the Joker and Barbara. Its hulking feet just missed the new commissioner.

"Joker!" cried Batman.

"Um, excuse me?" Barbara said. "I was just about to—"

"Push the Bat-Signal?" Batman cut her off. "Good call. I like your instincts."

He stomped his Scuttler past Barbara and towered over the Joker.

"Oh, Batman's here," the Joker practically sang. He had Rogues crowded all around him. "Wonderful!" His voice commanded attention. He made a sweeping circle, grinning at the crowd. "I've got a surprise for you guys, and it's going to make you SMILE."

"Uh-oh," said Batman. "His smile is our grimace! Everyone, get down!"

"I . . ." the Joker began.

"Joker, no!" cried Barbara.

". . . surrender," the Joker finished. He held his hands, revealing that they were in handcuffs!

"What?" said Barbara.

"What?" said the crowd. "What did he say?"

"Uh, what did you just say?" Batman asked.

"I said, *I surrender,*" the Joker repeated.

"I'm sorry, my Bat-ears must be malfunctioning because it sounds like you're saying—"

"I surrender," the Joker said, rolling his eyes. "I don't know how much more clearly or melodramatically I can say it."

"Okay, you know what? Cool it," Batman said. "You're a criminal. You run, and I catch you. It's kind of how this thing goes."

"Ah, bop, bop, bop," the Joker said. "Not anymore, Batman! You were right, there is no 'us.' So

there's no point in me trying to fight you anymore. This relationship doesn't mean anything. *Right?*"

There was a long silence as Batman and the Joker stared at each other.

"Ohhh, I get it," said Batman at last. "You're up to something."

"I am not up to anything," the Joker said calmly. "I just want to go to Arkham Asylum for all my crimes." He blinked innocently.

"I don't believe you for a minute," said Batman, shaking his head.

"Okay, Batman," said Barbara. "We'll take it from here."

"Take what from here?" asked Batman. "None of it is real."

"Oh yes, it is!" said the Joker. "We're all surrendering, right, guys?"

"YEAH!!!" cried the Rogues.

"All right, listen up!" Barbara hollered. "All of you have the right to remain silent."

"Yeah!!" cried Bane.

"Meow, meow!" cheered Catwoman.

"Awesome," said Man-Bat.

"We're going to jail!" said Clayface.

Outside the ballroom, a reporter was broadcasting live. "This just in. The Joker and the Rogues have just arrested themselves."

Barbara led the Rogues out to a giant van with barred windows. As they followed her, they chanted happily, "We're going to jail! We're going to jail!"

Barbara pushed the Joker into the backseat of the van.

"Thank you!" the Joker said cheerfully.

Batman hurried to the other side of the car and pulled the Joker out of the opposite door. "Yeah, watch your head, Joker!"

"Ow! Batman!" the Joker scolded him, rubbing his head.

"Excuse me, what are you doing?" Barbara inquired.

"I'm Batman-ing," Batman explained.

"That's . . . not a thing," said Barbara, folding her arms.

"Yeah it is," said Batman. "This is the part where you chill out and wait for me to come back with a few clues while I take the Joker back to the Batcave for a little conversation."

"You're not taking the Joker anywhere," Barbara said firmly. "I'm in charge now. Barbara Gordon, new police commissioner. Nice to meet you."

Batman grinned. "Hey, girl."

"We're going to change the way we do things around here," said Barbara. "We're going to do the

right thing and take the Joker to Arkham Asylum for questioning . . . *together.*"

"Together," Batman repeated.

"Yeah, together," said Barbara Gordon.

"Oh, I get what you're saying," Batman replied, nodding his head.

"Great," Barbara said.

"Wink," said Batman, giving her his coyest wink.

"Wink?" Barbara replied, raising an eyebrow.

"Yeah," said Batman. "You have a crush on me, don't you?"

"Not even remotely." Barbara looked Batman in the eye.

Batman chuckled. "Oh. Yeah. Sure."

Barbara sighed. "Listen. You have a history and a relationship with the Joker that's valuable."

"Oh, does he?" asked the Joker, his voice oozing with sarcasm.

"Don't encourage him," Batman told Barbara.

Barbara went on as if Batman and the Joker hadn't interrupted her. "So follow me to Arkham Asylum, and we can BOTH interrogate him so we can save the city and get the bad guy. What do you say, Batman?" She extended a hand to him. "Will you work with me?"

"NO!" Batman snapped. "The Joker wants to go to Arkham Asylum. That's the last place he should want to go. Unless—ding, ding, ding, ding—he's got some big plan."

As Batman and Barbara bickered, Harley Quinn snuck through the crowd around them. She popped off her pigtails and popped on a new hairpiece and a pair of glasses. Then she emerged at Barbara's side.

"What if you put him in the Phantom Zone?" Harley Quinn asked, trying to sound like an innocent bystander.

"I'm sorry, what?" Batman asked, surprised.

"The Phantom Zone," Harley Quinn–in–disguise repeated.

"The Phantom Zone! That's a great idea," Batman declared.

"You're welcome, Batman," said Harley. "I'm just a concerned citizen." She winked at the Joker and melted back into the crowd.

"You bet you are," replied Batman, not really thinking of anything but his new plan.

"Wait! If we put him in the Phantom Zone, then we'll DEFINITELY never figure out what his plan is," Barbara objected.

"Yeah, but then he'll be locked up for good, so

problemo solvedo," said Batman dismissively. He yanked Joker out of the prison van again. "Come on, Joker!"

"Batman, what are you doing? Seriously?" she yelled. "Batman, put the Joker down!"

"No."

"Yes!"

"No."

"Yes!"

"No!"

"Officers!" Barbara commanded the police officers to stop Batman.

The officers moved in, surrounding the Caped Crusader.

"Smoke bomb!" Batman cried. He threw a smoke bomb into the air.

When the dust cleared, Batman was gone.

10

Fuming! Batman was fuming! And it wasn't from the smoke bomb he'd used to escape the scene with Barbara Gordon.

No, Batman was fuming mad! He was fuming mad because Barbara Gordon had refused to let him deal with the Joker on his own terms.

Who did she think she was? Did she think it was her job to make decisions about how criminals should be punished? Geez, the new police commissioner had a lot of nerve.

But thanks to the concerned citizen at the scene, Batman knew what to do with the Joker. He needed to send that green-haired bad guy to the Phantom Zone.

Now, Batman didn't know very much about the Phantom Zone. The Phantom Zone was another dimension. It wasn't a place on Earth at all. It was like a cosmic prison out in space.

Even though Batman was sure about his plan, he had no idea how to send someone to this otherworldly place. Luckily, Batman had a supersmart Computer to do his research for him.

The moment Batman returned to the Batcave, he called, "Computer! How do I put the Joker in the Phantom Zone? I need the quickest route, no freeways."

Batman waited for a moment. But Computer did not reply.

"Computer, do you hear me?" he demanded.

Batman was so preoccupied with his new mission, he didn't notice that Alfred was sitting right behind him.

"Hello, Master Bruce," his butler greeted him.

"Alfred, there's something wrong with Computer. Watch this: Computer!"

When nothing happened, Batman tried again, louder this time. "See? Nothing! Computer!"

Again, the typically prompt Computer failed to respond.

"You see what I'm saying?" Batman said to Alfred.

"There's nothing wrong with it, sir," Alfred tried to reassure Batman. "I've just taken away your computer privileges." He pointed to Computer's screen, which was frozen by a parental lock.

Batman's jaw dropped. "The parental lock? You can't do that," he declared.

"Oh, I can," Alfred said with certainty. "I've been reading 'Setting Limits on Your Out-of-Control Child.'"

"You know what? It doesn't matter because I have a double-secret, super-password that unlocks the parental lock." Batman had a smug smile on his face.

"You mean 'thejoker_stinks'?" Alfred wondered.

Gasp! Batman's smug smile disappeared.

"I changed it," said Alfred.

"Come on, Alfred," Batman pleaded. "I need to stop the Joker. How am I supposed to do that without Computer?"

"Sir, it's time for you to stop this unhealthy behavior."

"No, it's not."

"You need to take responsibility for your life," Alfred tried to explain.

"Not right now, I don't." Batman scowled for emphasis. He wasn't in the mood to be responsible, not in the way Alfred meant.

"And it starts by raising your son." Alfred looked Batman in the eye.

There was a pause. A very long pause.

"I'm sorry," Batman replied at last. "I literally have no idea what you're talking about."

"The young orphan you adopted at the gala, remember?" Alfred motioned to a video monitor, which showed a boy running through the halls of Wayne Manor. It was Dick Grayson, the awkward kid from the orphanage—the same one who had asked Bruce Wayne endless questions about top strategies for getting adopted.

Right now, Dick was singing a rendition of an R & B tune. He had a sweet voice but was somewhat off-key.

"Do you remember, Master Bruce?" Alfred asked.

"I adopted a kid at the gala?" Batman mumbled with disbelief. "I thought I was being sarcastic." He looked at the screen again.

Now the kid was sliding down the grand entrance hall's well-polished bannisters.

"Whee!" Dick exclaimed as he dismounted. "Hello, suit of armor," he greeted the empty metal suit. "*En garde!*" Dick pantomimed swordplay, unaware that anyone was watching him.

"Well, he's here now," Alfred said, a sly smirk playing with the corners of his mouth.

"Hello, table!" Dick said with enthusiasm.

"And I must say I've grown rather fond of the young lad," Alfred added.

"Hello, secret camera!" Dick waved at the camera.

"You should get to know him," suggested Alfred.

"Yeah, I've got time for that," Batman replied in a flat tone.

"You do?"

"I'm being sarcastic again," Batman insisted.

"But you and he have a lot in common," Alfred said.

"Hello, family photos," the boy said, standing in front of the photo gallery.

"He lost his parents at a very young age," Alfred explained.

Batman watched the boy as he stared at the wall of Wayne family photos.

"I've always wanted one of these," Dick's voice turned suddenly serious.

"Two people don't need to be related to share the unmistakable bond between father and son," Alfred said seriously. "Am I right, Batman?"

Batman studied Dick closely. "Alfred?" he said at last.

"Yes, sir?" Alfred replied hopefully.

"You've been watching too many made-for-TV movies," he said.

"Oh," said Alfred. He tried to hide his disappointment.

"Whatever you're trying to do here, it's very cute," Batman went on.

"Thank you, sir," Alfred replied.

"But I'm the boss, and you're the butler, so I'm going to go fight crime while you put the kid on the next jet back to the orphanage."

"As you wish, sir," said Alfred. He turned away, then stopped and pulled out his duster. "Whoops-a-daisy," he said, "accidentally" brushing against a lever.

Clink! The door to the Batcave slid open.

"Wait, what are you doing?" Bruce asked, horrified.

"Dusting," Alfred said innocently.

"You can't let him into the Batcave!" Batman protested.

"I'm not," his trusted butler replied. "I'm letting him into your life."

11

Dick Grayson was a curious lad. Since he was already busy exploring Wayne Manor's extensive library, it didn't take him long to discover the secret entrance to the Batcave. Who wouldn't want to slide down one of those fabulous poles like a fireman? "Ohhhhh!" he yelled as he zipped down. "Wheeeeee!"

But when he landed, he found himself someplace far cooler than a fire station. He was in a dark cavern. He gasped as he stepped through the massive door. "WHAT?!? IT'S THE BATCAVE?!" he cried.

Dick stepped in reverently, looking around in disbelief.

"Oh my gosh, oh my gosh, oh my gosh, oh my gosh, oh my gosh, oh my gosh, oh my gosh, oh my gosh, oh my gosh!" Dick cried. Then he noticed all the amazing vehicles that could only belong to one person . . . er, Super Hero.

"EEAAHHHGGGHHHH!!!" Dick wailed when he realized where he was. He was so busy taking in all the fabulous stuff that he wasn't watching where he was going. That's how he walked straight into Batman.

"Uhhh! Batman? Whoa!"

"You're darn right, whoa," Batman replied.

"Wait. Does Batman live in Bruce Wayne's basement?" Dick asked, trying to piece it together.

"No, Bruce Wayne lives in Batman's attic," the Caped Crusader replied.

A huge smile spread across the newly adopted kid's face. "We can have sleepovers every night!"

"No, we can't," Batman insisted.

"Wow, look it's the Bat-Sub!" Dick announced, pointing.

"Wait, don't touch that," Batman ordered.

"And over there, it's the Bat Space Shuttle!"

"Please keep your hands off that," the Super Hero advised.

"Oh!" Dick looked up. "It's the Bat Zeppelin."

"Don't touch that, either."

"It's the Bat-Train!"

"No."

I'm Batman, and I'm here to tell you all about how I saved Gotham City from the Joker's biggest plot ever. I also made a whole bunch of new friends along the way.

It all started when the Joker attacked the Gotham City Energy Plant. I defeated him for like the millionth time . . . and he got a little bummed out when I told him he wasn't my greatest enemy.

I went home to hang out in the Batcave with Alfred, my butler and father figure.

Alfred reminded me that I'd said I'd go to a retirement party for Jim Gordon, Gotham City's Police Commissioner. I got to show off my new threads!

At the party, my alter ego, Bruce Wayne, met this orphan, Dick Grayson. The kid was so cool, Bruce ended up adopting him!

Then the mayor introduced us to the new police commissioner, Barbara Gordon.

That's when the Joker and his Rogues burst into the party. This was a job for Batman!

Barbara Gordon wanted to put the Joker in Arkham Asylum. But I knew about a better place for him—a prison called the Phantom Zone.

But first, I had to get the Phantom Zone Projector—and I needed a little help from my new son to get it.

The Joker's plan was a bit more complicated than I thought. I had to get a little help to stop him.

This is Barbara as Batgirl.

And this is Dick as Robin.

Working together, we took down the Joker!

"It's the Bat Kayak!"

"No."

"It's the Bat Dune Buggy!"

"No."

"It's the Bat—Shark Repellent?"

"Uh, actually, you can touch that," Batman relented. "It's completely useless."

"Whoa, thanks, Batman!" Dick picked it up and tenderly examined the spray bottle.

Alfred quietly approached with his broom. He whistled as he worked, looking quite content.

Batman considered the kid's position, a little too close to Computer's terminal. "Now just stand over there, and don't touch, look, or do anything for the remaining moments you have in my presence," he directed.

"Okay, cool," replied Dick.

As soon as Dick was out of the way, Batman rushed to the terminal.

"Computer!" he called out.

"Go ahead," stated Computer.

"How do I put the Joker in the Phantom Zone?" Batman requested.

"The Joker can only be put in the Phantom Zone using the Phantom Zone Projector," said Computer. "Current location of the Phantom Zone Projector is at Superman's Fortress of Solitude. It is located deep inside the Atomic Cauldron. However, my analysis indicates only an object with a seven-centimeter circumference can enter the cauldron."

Batman measured out seven centimeters with his hands. It was very small. "I can't fit in there with these shoulders. I'm way too buff."

"Sad but true," Computer replied.

"That's my cross to bear," said Batman.

"Additionally, once inside the cauldron, multiple Kryptonian defense systems will engage. Chance of total mission failure is one hundred and ten percent."

"Those are not great odds," Batman admitted. He thought for a moment, hoping for an answer. For no apparent reason, a vision of Dick Grayson sliding down the Wayne Manor bannister flashed through his head.

"Wait a minute. Hey, kid!" he yelled to his newly adopted son.

"Yes, sir?" Dick responded, his voice full of hope.

"You're nimble, right?" Batman said.

"I sure am!" Dick replied.

". . . and small?" Batman asked.

"Very!"

". . . and quiet?"

"When I desire to be," Dick whispered, his eyes lighting up with mischief.

"And one hundred ten percent expendable," Batman added under his breath.

"I don't know what that means," Dick confessed. "But okay!"

Batman turned and led Dick out of the main room of the Batcave. "Great. Follow me."

Batman turned on his heel and led Dick away from Computer and into his costume room.

"Cool!" Dick said.

"Preparing mission gear," Computer stated.

"Wow, look at all these," Dick said, eyeing the endless number of Batsuits. He touched the sleeve of one before moving on to the next. And he watched as Batman suited up for the mission.

"Do I get a costume for the mission, too?" Dick asked.

"I got a feeling you'll just look like a kid on Halloween," Batman said, dismissing the idea. "Don't you think?" His costumes were all designed for a full-grown man.

Without asking, Dick turned on the electronic costume rack.

"Don't touch that!" Batman said.

But it was too late. The costumes were whirling by, each more elaborate than the last.

"Woo-hoo!" Dick yelped with joy. He had never seen so many shades of black, gray, slate, shale, granite, charcoal, navy, midnight, silver, and platinum in his life.

Computer announced each outfit as it passed: "The Mariachi."

"I like that one," said Dick.

"No, that's mine," Batman claimed.

"Clawed Rain," said Computer.

"Okay, that one?" suggested Dick.

"No way," said Batman.

"This one?" Dick asked as another costume circled past.

Batman shook his head. "Absolutely not."

"Anger Blade," Computer said. "Bubonic Boy."

Batman said no to them all.

"How's this?" Dick asked. "How do we feel about this one?"

Batman frowned. "Dress-up parties are for grown-ups only," he said.

"Wait, what's that one there?" Dick pointed excitedly to a yellow, green, and red number. It was very bright compared with many of Batman's somber suits.

"Oh, that was for an assignment called the Jamaica Caper," Batman replied. "The locals called me 'Reggae Man.'"

"I love it!" cried Dick, grabbing it off the rack. He fumbled as he tried to change clothing. He searched for the zipper and struggled with the buckle.

But when Dick looked in the mirror, he couldn't help but admire himself. "Oh, it feels like I was poured into this," he said, running his hand along the smooth fabric. "My only trouble is . . . these pants are just a little tight. I don't know if I could throw a kick or jump in them. I've got an idea . . ."

He reached down and ripped the legs right off the pants, making the uniform into shorts—really short shorts.

"That's better," Dick announced, shaking his hips. "Now I'm free, now I'm moving, come on Batman, let's get groovin'!" He did a few dance steps and kicked his heels in the air.

Batman glared back at him. "I can only look you in the eyes right now," he said, embarrassed.

Alfred walked in, still holding on to his duster. He looked at Batman and Dick with a combination of concern and confusion.

"Uh, sir, what are you doing?" he questioned.

"What do you mean?" Batman replied innocently.

"Why is Master Dick dressed like that?" the butler wondered.

"How dare you tell me how to parent my kid whom I just met!" Batman pretended to be offended, but he was just buying time. "To the Batmobile!"

"Hot diggity dog!" Dick exclaimed, scampering behind the Caped Crusader.

Computer responded at once. "Vehicle rotisserie engaged. Retrieving the Batmobile."

Batman jumped in behind the wheel.

"Atomic battery to power. Turbines to speed," announced Computer.

"Hey, kid, let's go," Batman said, glancing at Dick.

"Aw, shoot," the kid said, looking down at his feet.

"What?"

Dick's forehead wrinkled with worry. "I probably shouldn't leave until I get the thumbs-up from my new old man, Bruce Wayne," Dick explained.

"Uh, yeah," Batman responded, thinking quickly. "Well, here's the thing: Bruno and I decided to share custody of you. So I get a say, and you're mission approved." He gave Dick a thumbs-up and a big smile.

"No way!" Dick couldn't believe his good luck. "Is this really happening?"

"Yeah."

"Woo-hoo! A month ago I had no dads, then I had one dad, now I have two dads, and one of them is Batman!" Dick exclaimed.

"So, are you ready to follow Batman and learn a few life lessons along the way?" Batman asked.

"I sure am, Dad Two! But first, where's the seat belt?" Dick searched the crease of the seat, looking for a buckle.

"The first lesson," Batman replied, "is that life doesn't give you seat belts. LET'S GO!"

Batman pressed on the gas pedal, and the Batmobile surged forward.

As they exited the Batcave, an old lady walked directly in front of them, and Batman slammed on the brakes.

The Batmobile jolted to a stop, and Dick flew headfirst into the windshield with a *slam. OOF!*

"Oh my goodness. I'm so sorry!" Batman stammered. He reached over and lifted Dick by the armpits. "Get back up in that seat. There you go." He gave Dick a little pat on the head as he tried to determine if the boy was seriously injured.

Dick was still in pain and shock, but he didn't want it to show. He wanted to seem tough for his new dad.

"Hey, listen, as soon as I get back to the Batcave, I'll make sure Alfred puts seat belts on there. But for the time being, I'm just gonna put my arm right here." Batman reached his arm out in front of Dick, acting like a human barrier.

Dick forced a smile and nodded.

"And now, we're going to gently ease out of here ... and so here we go ... real gentle-like," Batman explained.

In what seemed like slow motion, The Speed-wagon gracefully transformed into the Batwing and eventually picked up speed before jetting off toward Superman's famous escape, the Fortress of Solitude.

12

Half an hour later, Batman landed the Batwing on an icy patch just outside of the Fortress of Solitude.

Dick could hardly believe they were outside the Man of Steel's secret hideout. It didn't look very much like a house—more like giant, diagonal slabs made out of icicles. Dick shivered.

Batman turned to his newly adopted son. "Okay, here's the plan," he began. "Like all Super Heroes, Superman has zero friends, and he spends most of his time basking in sweet, sweet isolation here at his 'alone palace.'"

One of the only things Batman admired about Superman was the fact that he had a getaway for being by himself, and he didn't try to hide it.

Superman had actually used the word *solitude* in the name of his place. Impressive.

"So," Batman continued, "I'll keep Superman busy while you sneak into that vent and get the projector." He pointed to a very narrow vent that was about half the size of a dog door—not even big enough for a Jack Russell terrier—barely big enough for a well-fed Chihuahua. "Got it?"

"Copy that!" Dick agreed, but then a thought occurred to him. "Oh, here's an idea! I could also go—"

"Don't even finish that thought," Batman said, shaking his head. "See this counter?" He pointed to a fancy watch on his wrist. He clicked a button until the screen said:

BATMAN: 5,678,483
EVERYONE ELSE: 0

"These are all the good ideas Batman has had, and this is everyone else," he explained. "No one else ever has any good ideas, so don't even try. Your superpower..." Batman paused for effect and checked to make sure Dick was listening. He was. "Your superpower is excellent listening skills and execution of my ideas. Let's try it out."

"You got it, Dad," Dick said cheerfully.

"And don't call me 'dad,'" said Batman. "Now, begin mission!"

"Yes, Papa," Dick replied.

Batman scowled. "Papa falls into the 'dad' category," he said disapprovingly. He turned away, his black cape rippling in the frigid breeze.

Batman approached the entrance to the Fortress of Solitude without looking back. When he got to the oversize door, he rang the doorbell. *Ding-dong.*

The door opened a crack, and Superman peeked out.

"Supes!" Batman greeted him.

"Batman?" Superman said in surprise. "What are you doing here?

"Don't worry about it, dog," Batman said. "I'm not here to throw down or anything."

"Yeah, I figured that out when you rang the doorbell," Superman pointed to the doorbell button. "Besides, I could crush you if you did."

Batman chuckled. "Yeah, sure, yeah . . . okay." Sometimes, Superman's sense of humor wasn't all that funny, but Batman was on a mission, so he had to go with it. "Listen, thank me later, but I just happened to be in the 'hood, and I figured that you could probably use the—"

Batman gave the door a little shove. He wasn't exactly inviting himself in, but Superman obviously was *not* getting the hint.

But as soon as the door swung open, Batman realized that Superman was not alone. He was throwing a raging party, and just about the entire Justice League was there: Wonder Woman, The Flash, Green Lantern, Aquaman, Martian Manhunter, and more.

They were all rockin' to the hip musical stylings of an awesome DJ. It was awkward for Batman to see the members of the Justice League dancing in their Super Hero uniforms. Had they no dignity?

But a better question was: Why were they all there? And the best question was: Why wasn't Batman on the guest list?

The music suddenly stopped, and everyone at the party turned to look at Batman—even the ultracool musical guest.

"—company," Batman finally completed his sentence.

No one said anything. Someone coughed, and the sound seemed to echo through the expansive entrance hall.

Batman's heart pounded in his throat. He could face evil villains in epic battles without raising his pulse, but just then he felt a layer of sweat break out on his upper lip.

"Wait a minute, what . . . ?" Batman took in the scene. These were his colleagues. Everyone there was in the good fight against the bad guys. "Are you having the . . ."

Batman had just caught sight of a big banner stretching from one side of the room to the other; it read 57TH ANNUAL JUSTICE LEAGUE ANNIVERSARY PARTY!

". . . the 57th Annual Justice League party . . . without me?"

More silence.

Now two people coughed.

The crowd of Super Heroes shook their heads.

"No," said Martian Manhunter.

"What?" said The Flash.

"Uh-uh," said Wonder Woman.

"No, dude," Superman spoke up, but his tone was unconvincing. "You were totally invited. *Right, guys?*"

"Oh yes," came a couple of weak voices from the crowd.

"Are you really doing this party without me?" he asked, looking first at Superman and then scanning the faces of the large crowd.

"No!" came several half-hearted denials. "We wouldn't do that!"

89

"You didn't get the invite?" Superman mumbled. "I guess there must have been some mistake with the email."

"Pretty sure you were cc'ed," said Aquaman. But Batman knew that Computer would have told him if he'd been invited to a big party like this.

"Yeah, check your spam folder, man," cried Gleek.

"Good point, Gleek," said Superman, putting his arm around Batman. "Well, I guess we can officially agree that clears that up! So enjoy the party, bro! Hit it, DJ Cyborg!"

The Flash hurried over. "Great, Batman's here!" He handed Batman a phone, and then motioned for the Justice League to huddle in close for a photo. "Can you take a photo of all of us?"

"Of all . . . you guys?" said Batman. "Uh, sure . . ."

"Thanks, man!" said The Flash, rushing into the frame. "Everyone, say 'SUPER FRIENDS'!"

"SUPER FRIENDS!" the members of the Justice League chorused as Batman took the shot.

"Let me see!" said The Flash. "Great! We got everyone! Thanks, Batman!"

"Uh, sure, no problem," Batman replied.

13

Meanwhile, young Dick Grayson was busy wriggling through the narrow space of the vent. He crawled ahead at a steady pace until he reached a hole that he could see through.

"Bat-Dad? Bat-Dad?" Dick said into his comm.

Batman touched the communication device on his ear. "Yeah?"

"If I'm going to be a Super Hero and go on awesome Super Hero missions like this one, can we use code names?" Dick asked.

"Let me see . . . no," said Batman flatly.

"Mine can be Robin!" said Dick eagerly.

"As in, the small, midwestern, frail bird?" Batman asked.

"Yeah, and I already have a catchphrase," Dick

said cheerfully. "You ready? 'Tweet tweet on the street.'"

"Hard pass," said Batman.

"And a song!" Dick said, zipping down a chute. "*Fly, Robin, Fly!*" he sang.

"Harder pass," said Batman.

Dick crawled out of the vent and entered a room deep inside the Fortress of Solitude. He jumped and flipped through the various booby traps, making it to a tunnel on the other side. Then he stopped short.

Laser beams crisscrossed the tunnel. Not even a mosquito could get through without tripping the alarm.

"Dad, I can see the target, but there's some kind of laser energy thing that I can't get through," Dick said.

"Okay, I'll see if I can shut it off," Batman replied. "But I'm going to have to make up an excuse in order to leave the party without anybody noticing . . ."

Batman stood alone on the edge of the room. All around him, there were people dancing, but no one seemed to notice him. He slid his back along the wall until he got to the door. "Bye," Batman said, ducking out.

Stealthily the Caped Crusader made his way

through the fortress's long hallways to the Knowledge Crystal Room. According to Computer, he'd be able to deactivate the laser-beam blockade there so Dick could access the Atomic Cauldron. The crystals were powering the beams that protected the tunnel.

Batman rushed over to the ring of crystals and considered the collection of gems, uncertain which one would do the trick. He selected one and held it up to the light.

"Tell me when the lasers are off, all right?" he directed Dick. Then he tossed the first crystal to the ground. It shattered into a thousand pieces.

"Now?" Batman asked.

"No," replied Dick.

"Now?" Batman asked, hurling another brilliant crystal to the ground.

"No," said Dick.

"How 'bout now?" Batman started to juggle them, and one dropped.

"Not quite," Dick answered.

"Darn it, it's gotta be one of these," Batman said, throwing them left and right. "Is it this one? Or this one?" When he tossed the last crystal, the laser beams turned off.

"Oh my gosh! You did it, *Padre*!" Dick exclaimed. "It's off!"

"Okay, now you've got to make your way through that obstacle course to the Atomic Cauldron. We need that Phantom Zone Projector."

"Ten-four," replied Dick.

"Now do everything I say," said Batman. He pulled up a video comm link on his wrist. It let him see everything Dick was doing. "Jump!"

Dick jumped from his platform, heading toward the Atomic Cauldron.

"Hold on. Do a front flip," Batman demanded.

Dick did as his new dad asked.

Batman barked a series of orders as Dick made his way through the deathly obstacle course. Obviously, Superman wasn't messing around. The Phantom Zone Projector was as tightly guarded as the top tech company's next phone upgrade.

But Dick was undaunted. The boy proceeded to do perilous acrobatic tasks, skirting booby traps on the left and then the right and then right in front of him.

"Do a backflip. Triple axel. *Plié. Relevé. Jeté*," Batman ordered.

Each time Batman barked out a command, Dick sprinted, dove, and contorted himself with absolute perfection. He was getting closer to the Atomic Cauldron.

"Pythagorean theorem," Batman said.

"A-squared plus B-squared equals C-squared," Dick answered.

"Physicalize it!" Batman demanded.

Dick did his best to illustrate the triangular theorem with his very nimble body.

"Great listening!" Batman said. "Jump! Hold! Hold! Now jump!"

Dick jumped, held, held, and jumped! He darted across a spinning cage and leaped through an opening. "*Fly, Robin, Fly!*" he sang as he jumped.

Dick sped through a long hallway, swinging and twisting his way past razor-sharp claws and other ominous-looking obstacles. Finally he was close enough to grab the projector! "Wooo-hooo!" he exclaimed. "I've got the projector, Dad!"

Batman clenched his fist in triumph. "Boo-yah!" he cried.

He headed back through the halls of the Fortress of Solitude. He returned to the party undetected. He walked casually through the room, expecting someone to approach him. But he sauntered through the groovin' group without anyone noticing. He made his way to the front door, slipped out, and met Dick by the Batwing.

"We did it!" crowed Dick, who'd had to crawl back through the cramped vent, this time carrying

the bulky projector. His voice was full of pride. "We did it! How'd I do?"

"I don't know to describe this feeling," Batman began, "but watching you . . . out there . . . seeing this whole thing through your eyes . . . well, it just made me feel so proud," he paused, "of myself."

"Oh, you're such a great dad!" Dick said with genuine affection. He put his arms out and took a big step toward Batman.

Batman pressed his hand against the boy's forehead to stop him.

"What are you doing?" Batman inquired.

"I'm trying to give you a big ol' hug," Dick explained. "That's how I hug all my buddies at the orphanage."

"You know what?" said Batman. "You just reminded me of something very important when you said that word."

"What word, *hug*?" Dick asked.

"Nope," said Batman. "*Orphanage.* Now hop in."

And together, Batman and Robin took off in the Batwing.

14

Ten minutes later, the Batwing was circling above the orphanage.

Batman hit the brakes, and the Batwing screeched to a stop. Batman popped open the cockpit.

"Well, this is you," he said with forced cheerfulness. "The ol' orphanage."

"Oh," said Dick sadly. "I guess this can only mean one thing." He took a step out onto the wing.

"Yeah," said Batman.

"I'm getting a brother?" said Dick hopefully.

"Uh, no," said Batman.

"A sister?" Dick said, his voice as chipper as could be.

Batman took a deep breath. "No, it means that,

um . . . kid, sometimes, in this world, you've got to accept—"

Batman looked down into Dick's eyes. The kid was gazing up at him, his eyes glistening with hope and adoration.

"You've got to accept that sometimes . . ." Batman tried to go on. "That sometimes . . . you've got to check your grappling gun!" he finished. He quickly aimed a hook at Dick, pulling him back into the cockpit.

"Woo-hoo!" cheered Dick.

"Yeah. Totally works," said Batman. "Okay. Good." He handed the Phantom Zone Projector back to Dick. Then he kicked the Batwing into gear again and headed for Arkham Asylum.

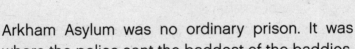

Arkham Asylum was no ordinary prison. It was where the police sent the baddest of the baddies. Arkham Asylum housed the most evil criminal masterminds.

The building was a spookfest. With its Gothic spires and rickety iron gate, it looked like a haunted house that had been condemned because it was too scary.

As he and Batman dashed up the asylum's

front steps, Dick looked up at the building and shuddered. He tightened his grip on the Phantom Zone Projector.

"C'mon, kid," Batman said.

Just as they reached the main entrance, Barbara Gordon stepped out. "Batman...," she said in surprise.

"Barbara! Hey there," said Batman. "Look at you."

"Who's this?" she asked, indicating Dick.

"Hi, Ms. Gordon!" Dick said, waving cheerfully.

"Is that your son?" Barbara asked.

"Yes, I am!" Dick answered quickly.

"No! That's just weird," Batman said.

"It's weirder if he's not your son," Barbara pointed out.

"Right," said Batman hurriedly.

"Batman," said Barbara.

"Yes?" said Batman.

"Why is your not-son trying to smuggle the Phantom Zone Projector into Arkham Asylum?"

"Um, Barbara, look out!" With that, Batman threw a smoke bomb. "Go, go, head for the elevator, now!" he hissed to Dick. He grabbed his not-son's hand and together they sprinted past the guards into the asylum.

Barbara coughed and waved smoke away from her face. "Guards! Code Red," she shouted into

her walkie-talkie. "Batman and his child accomplice are trying to infiltrate the Joker's cell!"

"Copy that, Commissioner," was the response.

Inside, the loudspeaker crackled to life. "Attention all inmates! We're on high alert. Return to your cells immediately!"

One inmate was happy to hear this announcement. "Hee, hee, hee, hee, hee," the Joker giggled to himself. He was sitting in his cell, twiddling his thumbs. His plan was coming together. Even he was surprised at just how cunning he could be.

Batman was coming for him. And the Joker was willing to bet not on black, but on the fact that Batman would be bringing the Phantom Zone Projector with him.

Batman and Dick raced through the asylum before dive-rolling into the elevator. When Batman looked over his shoulder, he saw Barbara Gordon and her best officers charging after them.

"Seal off the perimeter!" Barbara cried.

"Yes, ma'am!" replied a guard.

Batman punched the CLOSE DOOR button, and they headed for the cellblocks.

On the ground floor, a small team of guards was waiting for them. They had their weapons aimed at the elevator doors.

When the elevator clanked to a stop and the doors opened, smoke spilled into the hallway.

"Freeze! Stop! Put your hands up!" demanded the guards.

But when the smoke cleared, no one was there.

"What?" the guards gasped as they stepped in the elevator, mystified.

"Ceiling drop!" Batman yelled as he and Dick dropped from above, knocking over everyone below.

Batman brushed the dust from the smoke bomb off his sleeves. "I can't believe you guys still don't check the ceiling," he said, shaking his head.

"But Dad," Dick paused to ask, "why are those guards chasing us?"

"It's a training exercise," Batman explained. "These guys are my bros. Go ahead and take a couple of them out."

As he spoke, a new team of guards rushed at them from the other end of the hallway. Batman threw Batarangs at a few of them.

"Hey, Frank!" he called out in a friendly fashion. "Good catch, Barney!" he cheered as he punched another in the jaw. The guard crumpled to the ground.

Dick decided to give it a try. "You want a piece of me, Bill?" he demanded, taking out a guard.

"See? They're all cool with it," Batman told Dick. "Let's go!"

Together Batman and Dick headed for the Joker's cell.

Batman spotted the Joker's bright-green shock of hair from across the cellblock. But the Joker was disappearing—behind a cell door. The doors were just inches from locking, and Batman was a hundred feet away.

With a snap of his wrist, Batman flung a Batarang across the cellblock. The Batarang wedged its way into the door just before the lock latched, jamming it open.

Batman swung across the divide with a grappling hook, landing right in front of the Joker's cell.

"'Sup, Joker," he greeted the villain.

"Hi, Bats," said the Joker cheerfully. "What brings you to Arkham Asylum?"

"Cut the baloney," Batman said. "I'm here for you!"

"You sure did go to a LOT of trouble for little old me," said the Joker coyly.

Batman nodded. When he spoke, his voice took on an official tone, as if he were a bailiff in a court of law. "All rise. The case of *Bat versus Joke* is now in sesh." He leaned in like a lawyer. "So let

me ask you something right off the 'bat.' Are you up to something?"

"Yes, I am," the Joker admitted.

"Case closed," Batman said grimly. "I hereby sentence you to be shot up into the Phantom Zone!"

Barbara Gordon was closing in on Batman. She reached the cellblock floor just in time to hear Batman's last words. "Oh no!" she cried. She couldn't believe it. She couldn't believe Batman would go against her and the police like this.

"Ooh, the Phantom Zone," the Joker said, his voice dripping with drama. "Puh-leeaaase! Don't banish me to that notorious space prison that houses all the universe's greatest villains!"

"That's it! That's his plan!" cried Barbara.

Batman lifted the Phantom Zone Projector and took aim at the Joker. "You're about to get served . . . your sentence."

"Batman, don't do it!" Barbara yelled, but it didn't matter. Batman's mind was made up.

"Case dismissed," Batman said, making sure the projector was properly lined up.

When he pulled the trigger, the projector shot out a laser blast so strong it threw him backward. The beam shot across the cell and straight at the

Joker, zapping the green-haired goon with a blinding burst of energy. There was a sound like thunder and several blasts of hot white light.

"Whhhoooaaaa!" yelled the Joker, his shrill voice fading away.

When the light cleared, the Joker was gone.

Batman felt a rush of victory. He threw black confetti over his head and blew a party horn in celebration. "Yeah, that's what I call saving the city again!" he crowed.

"You are an inspiration!" said Dick.

Batman and Dick danced with joy until . . .

CLANK!

Barbara Gordon slammed the cell door shut and locked it—with Batman inside!

"Batman, I can't believe you did this," said Barbara.

"You're welcome," said Batman.

"And even worse, you've made this kid an accessory to your crime," she said, shaking her head. She locked Dick into the cell next to Batman's. "Sorry, kid."

"That's okay," said Dick. "As long as I'm doing time in the big house with my old man, everything is going to be A-OK."

"May I request solitary confinement?" asked Batman.

Barbara Gordon took the Phantom Zone Projector from his grasp. "Officer, take this to the evidence locker room," she said, handing off the device to a security guard. "Keep it under twenty-four-hour armed guard until we can figure out how to get the Joker back."

"No problem, ma'am," the guard replied.

"Barbara, I just put the Joker in the *one* place where he can't do any more harm," Batman insisted.

"Yeah, but what if I'm right? What if you just gave the Joker exactly what he wanted?" Barbara replied.

"That is ridiculous," said Batman. "Why would anyone *want* to go to the Phantom Zone?"

15

Meanwhile, the Joker discovered he wasn't in Gotham City anymore. He was flying through a weird, space-like tunnel. It twisted and turned and seemed to go on far longer than possible. But at last, he landed. "Whoa!" he exclaimed.

"Welcome, super-villain!" said a stern voice. The voice belonged to the warden of the Phantom Zone. He was squat and looked oddly like a traffic light.

The Joker grinned. "Super-villain. That's good. This guy gets me," he said under his breath.

"What's your name?" asked the warden.

"It's the Joker."

"Great. Here's your toothbrush and cot," the warden said, placing a toothbrush in the Joker's

hand. "Do yourself a favor and find a good place to sleep, because you're going to be here for the rest of eternity. Bye." Then the warden was gone.

"Hey, take a look at the new guy," came a deep, dark voice from the shadows.

"I guess they'll just let anybody in here," said another.

"What? Are you serious? I'm the Joker. I'm the baddest bad guy in Gotham City," the Joker insisted, looking around at the nastiest monsters and no-good evil meanies he'd ever seen. These were the other inmates of the Phantom Zone, and they had "villain" written all over them. Scales, claws, drool, red eyes, icky smells, and downright nasty expressions.

"You don't look like a bad guy," growled one monster. "You look like an eggplant."

The other villains exploded in laughter, but the Joker was not daunted.

"Oh, eggplant. You're talking about me because of the green and purple . . . that's a good joke." The Joker chuckled. "Sorry, I'm just so FIRED UP about being here! I mean, you've got evil wizards; you have wicked witches; and, oh my, dragon beasts. I am such a geek for you all! I love your rampaging. And, since I'm here, maybe I can get some advice on how to defeat Batman."

"What is a Batman?" asked one villain.

"Batman is a pretentious guy who dresses up like a bat, and he's my greatest enemy. Well, I know he is, but he won't admit it," the Joker explained.

The villains listened closely. They murmured in agreement.

"Typical heroes. Always making it about themselves," another villain replied.

Now all the villains had something to add, a story to share.

The Joker grinned. His plan was proceeding even better than he'd dared to dream! Being sent to the Phantom Zone was the best thing that had ever happened to him! He had always wanted a mentor, someone to teach him to be more evil. Now he would have the advice of the greatest villains of all time!

And in the meantime, his best gal pal Harley Quinn was back in Gotham City with an ace up her sleeve . . .

Down in Arkham Asylum, three armed guards were transporting the Phantom Zone Projector to a secure room. They boarded an elevator headed toward the vault.

"Hey, did you see the game last night?" the first guard asked.

"Oh man, that was the craziest game I've ever seen in my life," the second guard answered. "Could you believe that coach? He was screaming, so angry . . ."

"You didn't see the game, did you," the first guard said.

"Nope," the second guard said sheepishly. "I'm new in town and I'm just trying to make friends!"

The elevator stopped, and a woman dressed in a white lab coat stepped on.

"Going up, ma'am?" the second security guard asked.

"No, but you're going down!" the woman said. "Hi-ya!"

The woman popped off her blond hairpiece. It was Harley Quinn! She whipped her mallet through the air, taking out both guards. Then she grabbed the Phantom Zone Projector and raced away.

Harley Quinn had spent some time in Arkham Asylum, and she knew just where to go. She headed for the stairs and took them two at a time.

Moments later, she was outside on the roof, with all of Gotham City stretching before her.

Harley Quinn smiled. Then she pressed a button on the projector's handle.

"Export options. Release inmate 'Joker.' Are you sure?" the projector computer asked.

"Yes, I am," said Harley.

"Please don't," said the computer.

But she did. "Release the Joker!" cried Harley Quinn.

The projector's beam brightened the night sky, and the power of the laser made the ground shake. A bright light shot up toward the sky. Then there was a zapping sound . . . and the Joker suddenly materialized beside Harley!

"Welcome back, sugarplum," she greeted him warmly.

The Joker grinned. Thanks to Harley's help, he'd finally outwitted Batman. Not only was he out of jail, but he had possession of the Phantom Zone Projector!

The Joker and Harley strode back through the halls of Arkham Asylum with their heads held high.

Harley held the ring of prison keys high in the air and jangled them. "Who wants a get-out-of-jail-free card?" she called in a singsong voice.

"Look, the boss is back!" the Riddler said, his hands wrapped around the cell bars.

"Wooooo-hoo!! Yay!" cheered the Rogues.

It only took a few minutes to unlock the cell door of every last Rogue.

Only when the criminal crew had poured onto the street, free of the Asylum walls, did Harley breathe a sigh of relief. "Now what does everyone say?"

"Thank you, Harley," the Rogues all answered.

"You're welcome," Harley Quinn answered, with a curtsy. "I'm happy to break you out of jail so we can all take over Gotham City together."

"Thank you, sugarplum. I couldn't have said it better myself," said the Joker. "You know recently, someone very mean and hurtful . . . Batman! . . . told me that I was not his greatest enemy, and that I would never take over the city. But I'm not the type to let a Negative Nelly tell me what I can and can't do. I'm more of a 'try and try again' kind of guy."

The Rogues all grumbled in agreement.

"While I was in the Phantom Zone, I learned a thing or two about being a super-villain," the Joker went on. His grin stretched all the way across his face and up to his eyes. "Here's the new Gotham City Takeover Plan: We take control of the energy plant tomorrow night. This time, we don't tell anyone, and this time we don't mess it up! We just blow it and everything within twenty miles to

smithereens. And if anyone tries to get in the way, I'll zap them with this!"

Harley placed the Phantom Zone Projector in the Joker's outstretched hands.

"Even Batman can't stop us now," the Joker boasted. "We are going to take this sad little town DOWN." He waved the projector above his head triumphantly. "But first, we will master the plan in our new hideout fortress. I propose Wayne Manor. As the nastiest villains, we deserve the fanciest digs!"

With that, the band of merry, menacing Rogues followed the Joker into the night.

16

Barbara Gordon was pulling another late night in her office when the two security guards from the elevator burst in.

"Ma'am, Harley Quinn just beat us up and took the Phantom Zone Projector!"

"I knew it!" said Barbara. She jumped up and ran to the door. "It's the Joker. He's back!"

Chief O'Hara was right behind the guards. "Harley Quinn and the Joker just let all the Rogues out of their cells! Commissioner, we have to put up the Bat-Signal."

"Um, let's say Batman couldn't receive the Bat-Signal right now," said Barbara. "What's plan B?"

"The Bat-Phone," O'Hara replied.

"Plan C?" Barbara asked, wincing.

"The Bat Fax Machine," the chief answered.

Barbara took a deep breath. "Do we have any strategies for defending the city that are not Bat-related?"

"Uh . . . no," said the chief.

"Okay," said Barbara. "I know what to do. We have to get the Phantom Zone Projector back."

Early the next morning, on Wayne Island, Alfred was sweeping the front stoop when he heard the rev of mighty engines. High-octane whoops and hollers followed.

It was the Rogues, coming to claim Wayne Manor as their new headquarters.

"Good grief," Alfred said. He dropped the broom, jumped into Bruce Wayne's limo, and raced away.

As he headed toward Arkham Asylum, Alfred attempted to avoid the hot spots of mayhem that were flaring up all over Gotham City. Croc . . . Catwoman . . . the Riddler . . . Captain Boomerang . . . the Rogues were attacking in small bands, wreaking havoc everywhere. Explosions seemed to come from every other block, and the stench of burnt rubber hung in the air.

Alfred shook his head. There was only one person who could help them now, and as far as his butler knew, he was locked up in Arkham Asylum.

Alfred stepped on the gas.

On the cellblock, Batman and Dick were standing by their cell doors. Each was leaning his head against the bars. And they were . . . singing?

"Kid!" Batman cried. "I said no harmonizing!"

"Sorry, Bat-Dad," said Dick. "I couldn't resist."

Suddenly, there was a loud screeching sound. Batman looked down at his arm. "The Bat Fax!" he gasped as a long scroll of paper shot out of his bicep armor.

There was a single item on the paper: the bat-symbol.

"The city needs me!" Batman said. "Hey!" he called to the closest guard. "Excuse me, can you get the commissioner and show her this?"

But the guard didn't have to go anywhere, because Barbara was already there. "Batman," she said coolly. "I sent you that fax. I hate to say this, but you're right. The city needs you."

"Yes! Let me out," said Batman.

"I'm only going to let you out on one condition," said Barbara.

"Name it," said Batman.

"You can't do it by yourself," she said. "The city is in so much trouble. No one could do this alone."

"UGGHHHH!" Batman cried. "Fiiiiinnnne. Who do I have to work with? The Teen Titans? The Omega Men? Young Justice?"

"No," said Barbara. "Me."

Batman was puzzled. "Just to be clear . . . this is a date, right?"

"Not at all," said Barbara, rolling her eyes. "You and I need to work together. Starting now."

"I want to help, too!" cried Dick from the cell next door.

"Kid, you're supposed to be on my side . . . when it comes to the fact that nobody should be on my team," Batman said patiently.

"And I shall join as well," said Alfred, joining Barbara outside the cell.

"How . . . did you get in here?" Barbara asked.

"Alfred Pennyworth. At your service, ma'am," Alfred said politely.

"Alfred! You've got to let me out of here," said Batman.

"Sir, the Joker and his accomplices have invaded the Batcave," Alfred said significantly.

"You'll never be able to defeat them all alone," said Barbara. "Especially if they have all your gear now," she added as an afterthought, glancing at Alfred.

"You know what I'm going to say, right?" said Batman.

"And it'll be more fun if we all do it together," said Dick.

"Well, that's majorly up for debate, but if we're being real," said Batman, "accepting help from an old man, a kid in his underwear, and a desk jockey—"

"So rude!" cried Barbara.

"—is kind of a bad look for Batman," Batman finished.

"Really?" said Barbara. "What's the worst that could happen? What are you so afraid of?"

Batman didn't answer right away. He looked at Alfred, and then looked away quickly.

"I'm not afraid of anything!" he said defensively.

"Okay, prove it," said Barbara. She unlocked his cell, and then Dick's.

"Okay, I will," said Batman, hurrying out of the

cell and then down the cellblock. The others followed him.

"Know what the B-A-T in Batman stands for?" Batman asked as they strode along the halls of Arkham Asylum.

"Best At Tantrums?" Barbara quipped.

"Funny," said Batman. "No. It stands for Best At Teamwork. Best At Teamwork Man is my full name."

"Hey, Teamwork-Man, maybe you can call the Justice League for help," Barbara suggested.

"No problemo," said Batman. "I've got them on speed dial." He punched in a long string of numbers, whispering, "It's ringing."

He listened for a minute, and then ended the call. "It went straight to voice mail."

"Weird," said Barbara.

"No, no, it's not," Batman said, shrugging. "Let's go!"

The new team emerged from Arkham Asylum to find a city in chaos.

"The Joker's at Wayne Manor," said Dick.

"Guys, I know the fastest way through the city," Barbara said. "Follow me!"

She darted ahead of the group. Alfred and Dick fell in behind her, keeping the pace. But almost at once, Batman ran and caught up with Barbara, passing her.

"Batman, what are you doing?" Barbara asked in a loud whisper.

"Just following ahead of you," he answered.

"The phrase is 'following *behind* you,'" Barbara reminded him. She motioned for Batman to get behind her.

"Oh, right, right," Batman said, and he let Barbara take the lead. But he couldn't stop himself and surged forward again, edging just ahead of the new commissioner.

Barbara narrowed her eyes and increased her speed. She and Batman kept alternating who was in front, back and forth and back and forth.

"We're adorable together," Batman said, winking at her.

Barbara just rolled her eyes.

17

"Look out! Adversaries ahead," Alfred called.

"There are so many of them!" Dick cried.

He wasn't exaggerating. The streets were filled with Rogues. They were led by Harley Quinn, who was making merry mayhem with her mallet. Behind her were Clayface, Mr. Freeze, Bane, and dozens more.

"Batman, they're going to see us!" Dick went on.

"Don't worry, I know what you guys need," said Batman, pulling his merch gun out of his Utility Belt. "Fire in the hole! KABOOM!"

Kaboom!

"No way," Barbara said, but that didn't stop Batman.

Boom! Kaboom! Kaboom! Kaboom! Kaboom! Kaboom! Kaboom!

"Ew, seriously?" Barbara muttered, looking down at the new outfit Batman's merch gun had just dressed her in. It looked a lot like a purple-and-yellow tracksuit.

"You're next," Batman told Alfred. *Kaboom!* Instantly, Alfred was clothed in a classic costume that looked like it came from the Batman Museum.

"Ha-ha!" Alfred exclaimed. "The old blue and gray."

"Yeah, just like a real bat," Batman said.

"Hey!" Dick said. "I can wear my costume, too!"

"Well, luckily for us, you left your costume back at the Manor," Batman said.

Rip! It took Dick 0.95 seconds to rip off his everyday clothes and reveal his yellow-and-red-and-green "Reggae Man" costume underneath.

"Nope." Batman sighed. "Your costume is under your clothes. That's . . . perfect. You're going to have to get a shot from the merch gun, too."

"Sir, he's just a boy," Alfred interjected. "Maybe Master Dick should wear what he wants?"

"Uh, no," said Batman. "If he wants to be like Batman, then he's going to have to learn how to walk, talk, think, act, fight, dress, drive, eat, sleep, and snorkel like Batman. Copy that?"

Before Alfred or Dick could respond, a pack of penguins swarmed around them.

"The next part is going to require help from all of you," Batman said, kicking a penguin away.

"Great," Barbara said, relieved to finally be included in the plan.

"I need you to live stream this on social media," said Batman, tossing out smartphones. He assigned different platforms to Dick, Alfred, and Barbara.

"Seriously?" Barbara asked in disbelief.

"Copy that, Dad!" Dick answered.

Batman winked and smiled as Dick pointed the phone and shot a series of pics.

"While you guys do that," Batman said. "I'm going to fight them on my own! GAAAAAAHHH!" Batman let out a yelp as he stormed the penguins. With flying kicks, he knocked the first row down like bowling pins. But then another group swarmed him, waddling around his feet and tripping him up.

"Guys, let's go," Barbara commanded, seeing that Batman was outnumbered.

"No, you guys just stay back. I got it," Batman insisted, swatting at a whole colony of penguins. "See, it's even easier than usual," he said, panting.

Suddenly, they were all surrounded. Out of the shadows came Mr. Freeze, Catwoman, and the Penguin.

"Meow, meow," Catwoman said, flicking her tail.

"Uh-oh," Barbara Gordon muttered. Then she yelled, "Attack!"

Dick, Alfred, and Barbara leaped into the fray.

"This changes nothing," Batman insisted, bouncing Batarangs off the walls around them to keep Catwoman at bay.

"Come on, guys, let's do this!" Barbara said, rallying the troops.

"No, no, you're doing it wrong," Batman said, watching Barbara battle Mr. Freeze. "Kick him in the face," he directed. He stopped paying attention to the army of web-footed minions and just gave Barbara pointers. "Now hit him in the chest. Now hit him in the ribs. Now hit him in the solar plexus."

With Batman distracted, the Penguin joined the battle. He wrapped his umbrella around Batman's neck from behind, trying to drag him to the ground.

"When it rains, it pours, wouldn't you say, Batman?" the Penguin said with a chuckle.

"I can help, Dad," Dick yelled, arriving at Batman's side.

"Just help the others," Batman muttered, trying to pull the umbrella away.

"Are you sure? Because it looks like you can't breathe."

"This is my resting rage face," Batman grunted.

"I've got just the thing you need!" Dick said, whipping out his Bat Shark Repellent. "I know penguins are birds and not fish, but they are both marine animals," Dick reasoned as he aimed the spray for the Penguin's pinched face. "So let's give this a go!"

When the spray squirted right in his eyes, the Penguin squawked in pain. He dropped the umbrella and waddled away.

"Woo-hoo! I saved my dad's life!" Dick cheered.

"Well, I invented that product, so, technically, I saved myself," Batman said, trying to catch his breath.

The other fights were almost even: Barbara against Mr. Freeze and Alfred against Catwoman.

All of a sudden, Alfred bellowed, "Everyone, stop!"

Surprisingly, the bad guys came to a halt.

"Sneak attack!" Alfred announced in an excited whisper.

Catwoman let out a shocked hiss just as Dick leaped up and knocked her down with an acrobatic kick.

"Woo-hoo!" Dick exclaimed.

Barbara nabbed Mr. Freeze's ray gun and turned it on him. The villain was stunned cold.

"We need to get out of here," Barbara said, knowing that the Rogues would not stay knocked down for long. She reached for her grappling hook—only to discover it was made out of chocolate. The merch gun had given her sugar-coated Bat-gadgets!

Barbara heard the patter of tiny webbed feet approaching. The Penguin and his birds were returning. "Quick, Batman, throw me your grappling hook!" Barbara called.

Batman scowled. "You can't use mine, you might scratch it."

"Hurry up," Barbara advised. "We don't have time."

"Okay, fine," said Batman. Barbara yanked his grappling hook off his belt. On her first try, she got the hook to knock around a lamppost above their heads.

"Okay, guys, grab on!" she called.

The team latched themselves to Barbara, and they shot up into the air.

18

As soon as they'd reached safety, Batman quickly went into MasterBuilder mode. He directed everyone to gather bricks from the rubble on the sidewalk. "The Rogues must have come this way," he muttered. The Joker's crew left destruction in its path . . . as always.

"I think I hear something," Dick said. "Something coming."

"Start throwing me bricks!" Batman directed. "I need a four-by-six. Come on, quick."

Batman used his lightning-quick reflexes to place brick after brick with precision. The others watched in awe of his brilliant brick instincts and started to help, trying to keep up.

"A two-by-four, two-by-four," Barbara murmured.

"I need an elbow piece. I need a tile," Batman said, half talking to himself.

"Whoa, whoa, whoa, AHHH!" Dick exclaimed as the plan started to come together. Batman was building a new Batwing!

But an army of Rogues soon appeared on the horizon. The street below them began to vibrate as the army approached.

"Get in!" Batman cried, still placing bricks. Alfred, Barbara, and Dick all scrambled in as the Batwing began to lift off. Batman was seated in the cockpit.

"Woo! Great MasterBuilding, huh, Batman?" he said, patting himself on the back. "How are you guys feeling? Super comfortable and impressed?" Batman asked as the other three attempted to cram themselves into the tiny cockpit.

"Not really. Why'd you build this thing with only one seat?" Barbara asked.

"All official Bat-vehicles have one seat. Read the sign," Batman said, pointing.

NO COPILOTS read the sign on the dashboard.

Right now, Barbara would have settled for being a comfortable passenger. Dick was curled up in her lap and Alfred's elbow was in her face as they skimmed over the heads of the Rogue army.

"Now contort yourselves into impossible angles and enjoy the ride to Wayne Manor," Batman instructed. He pushed a few buttons and accessed Computer through the cockpit's control panel.

"Searching the route to Wayne Manor," Computer said, gliding over a wooded stretch of a city park. "We've got more Rogues up ahead—all the way up to Twenty-Sixth Street. They are everywhere. Also, sir, I have some bad news."

As the Batwing rose into the sky, a large neon amusement park appeared in the distance. Batman frowned. He didn't remember anything that looked like a cheap overgrown carnival in that part of town before.

But it wasn't an amusement park at all. It was Wayne Manor! The Joker had made some "improvements."

"What??" Batman stammered. "What have you done? Wayne Manor, my beautiful mansion on an island?!"

Batman flew closer for a better look. He winced as he saw Joker's Rogues pushing his fabulous cars—convertibles, roadsters, pickup trucks, and more—into the river.

And it kept getting worse. The Rogues had not only destroyed Wayne Manor, they had also

discovered the secret entrance to the Batcave. Batman's heart sank when he saw Rogues driving all the great Bat-vehicles right out of the secret tunnel to the Batcave.

The Batwing. The Bat Zeppelin. The Batcycle. The Bat Kayak. The Bat-Sub. The Bat Dune Buggy.

"That's all my stuff!" Batman yelled.

"We're in big trouble now," said Barbara with a sigh.

"I know. They're going to mess with my radio presets," Batman worried.

Inside Wayne Manor, the Joker was in his element. "Hahahahaha! Now I know where you get your cool gadgets," he cackled with glee. "And I'm going to use them against you!"

As Batman's Batwing flew past, a host of vehicles bombarded it. From the air, from the ground, from the water, they took aim. It took Batman's most strategic flying to dodge the barrage. The Rogues aimed all their fire at the new Batwing. And they sent drones in close to land on the wings and cut wires and cause mayhem.

Aboard the Bat Zeppelin, Two-Face took his time. He waited for the right moment to shoot the first heat-seeking missile. He flipped a coin. "Now!" he yelled, and his minion fired away. "And again!"

The Joker and Harley Quinn enjoyed their role as spectators. "This is so much better than tennis," the Joker said.

Inside the crowded Batwing cockpit, Batman's team had reason to worry. Computer began to issue warnings, her commanding voice promising impending doom. "Warning!" Computer said. "Missiles locked. Warning! Missiles locked. Warning!"

"Okay, this just got real," Batman murmured as he tried to avoid a direct hit.

"Warning," Computer continued. "Impact imminent!"

Computer was right. The Batwing was hit! "Engine two malfunction!" Computer announced as Batman struggled to keep the Batwing in the air.

The Joker laughed uncontrollably, slapping his hand on his knee as if he'd just heard a great joke.

"Warning. Engine Three fail. Warning. Engine Four fail." Computer just kept the good news coming.

"We can't hold them off much longer," Barbara Gordon declared, seeing the team of armored vehicles gunning for them.

"I've got this under control," Batman insisted.

"Don't worry, Batman. I'm a pilot. I'll fly the Batwing. You fix the engine," suggested Barbara.

"It's all good, Babs," Batman replied. "I've got my autopilot on." He used a piece of rope to fasten the controls into the right position.

"Autopilot?" said Barbara. "That's just a rope!"

"Exactly," said Batman. "And until I get back, the rope's in charge. Now strap on your seat belts!"

"Where *are* the seat belts?" Barbara asked as Batman crawled out onto the wing.

"Life doesn't give you seat belts!" Dick replied. "That's Bat-Dad's lesson number one!"

Out on the wing, Batman began to build. But he also had to duck to avoid the drones that were whizzing in from all directions. "Get off me!" he cried.

"Come on, Master Dick, we need to help him!" Alfred said, handing him a sack of Batarangs.

"I'm with you, Grandpa!" Dick replied.

Alfred and Dick opened the cockpit hatch to a rush of wind. They climbed out on the wings and whipped Batarangs in every direction. Incoming drones began to fall from the sky as Batman kept rebuilding the engines.

"Get off my dad!" Dick cried.

"Unhand him, you animatronic fiends!" Alfred cried.

"What are you two doing out here!" Batman

yelled. "Kid, you disobeyed me! You're on a time-out!"

"No, you're on a time-out, sir!" Alfred retorted.

"I am not on a time-out!" Batman cried.

"Yes, you are!"

"Un-time-out me RIGHT NOW!" Batman cried.

"Not until you un-time-out Master Dick!" Alfred called.

"Guys, you're all un-time-out-ed, we have incoming!" yelled Barbara from inside the cockpit.

"Okay, everyone, time-out off!" Batman cried.

"Woo-hoo!" cried Dick. "I've been parented!"

But his celebration was short-lived, because missiles were zooming toward them.

Both Dick and Alfred ducked, but just then the Batwing swerved violently, and they were thrown off-balance.

"Help!" Dick yelled as he hung on by his fingertips.

Alfred wasn't any better off. He was clutching the dome of the cockpit with one hand.

"Dick! Alfred!" Batman cried, not sure who to save first.

"Batman, I can help you!" cried Barbara.

"No! You protect the rope," Batman said. "I can save them both!"

"The rope is fine," said Barbara desperately.

"Don't worry about me, sir. Save Master Dick!" Alfred demanded.

"I'm fine. I'll just do some of my gymnastics moves," Dick said.

Just then, a blast hit the Batwing's tail, and the whole jet shook.

"AHHHHHH! I'm falling," said Dick, losing his grip.

Batman secured a grappling hook to the Batwing and dove after Dick. "Gotcha!" he declared. He quickly fired a grappling hook toward Alfred. "Hold on. Almost there," he said.

But just as Batman was about to reach Alfred, the Batwing shuddered violently, and Alfred lost his grip.

"Alfred!" Batman cried.

Alfred plummeted toward the ground.

"Nooooooo!" Barbara Gordon cried. "Move over, rope!" She grabbed the Batwing's controls and put the jet into a steep dive. She swooped down, catching Alfred and pulling Batman and Dick back into the cockpit.

"Barbara, that was incredible," Batman exclaimed. "The BatRope saved Alfred! Wow, those were some insane moves, BatRope!"

"Actually, sir, Ms. Gordon saved him," Computer said.

"What? You mean . . . without you . . ." Batman stared at the police commissioner, finally putting it together.

"Alfred would have been a goner," Dick said.

Batman considered this for a moment, but only a moment because another heat-seeking missile was hot on the Batwing's tail.

"Batman, we can do this," Barbara said. "Trust us."

"All right, I'm starting to get the hang of this 'team' stuff," Batman declared. "But we're getting torn apart up here. So if we're going to make it to Wayne Manor, I'm going to need help from all of you."

The team decided they wouldn't be able to land as long as the zeppelin was launching missiles. They needed to stop Two-Face before he blew up all of Gotham City.

Each member of the team had a task. Alfred, who'd been a tail gunner in the Royal Air Force, got in the turret to cover them from the rear. Dick, with his acrobatic skills, was in charge of knocking any incoming drones off the wings. Barbara, the crack pilot, was flying. And Batman directed.

"Barbara, here's what I need you to do," Batman said. "Fly us straight at that zeppelin."

"WHAT?"

"Didn't you say 'trust me' like ten seconds ago?" Batman reminded her.

"Okay. Let's do this," answered Barbara, pulling her flight goggles into place.

"Woo! We're really doing this!" yelled Dick.

The Batwing swooped underneath bridges and over houses, zooming toward the Bat Zeppelin.

"You got bad guys coming up on your three," said Batman, acting as Barbara's eyes and ears. "There's a Batcopter at six o'clock."

"I don't see him!" Barbara yelled. But Alfred, stationed at the back, did. He knocked the Batcopter from the sky with one shot.

"The Bat Kayak is directly below us, taking aim with a giant bazooka," Batman noted. "But keep heading toward the zeppelin."

Barbara stayed on target, even though she didn't understand the plan.

Inside Wayne Manor, the Joker was watching on a screen, and he didn't like what he was seeing. "Finish them off!" he screeched. "Bat Kayak," he said over the radio, "I want you to blast them out of the sky."

By this time, Dick had wriggled out onto the wing and was attempting to dislodge drones.

"More drones on two o'clock," Batman advised Dick, yelling over the manic whirl of wind.

"Great job, team," Batman told his crew. "It's like looking in three mirrors." It was a rare

compliment from the Caped Crusader. "Barbara, wait for my signal."

"Waiting on that signal," Barbara said, flying full throttle toward the zeppelin. She was feeling anxious.

"Don't worry. It's coming! Keep going! Keep going!" Batman insisted, checking the distance to the zeppelin and the aim of the Bat Kayak from below.

"Batman!" Barbara yelled. The Batwing was practically on top of the zeppelin now.

The Joker, watching on screen, called for the launch of the Bat Kayak bazooka. "Fire!" yelled the Joker.

"Now, Barbara! Dive-bomb!" yelled Batman.

Everything happened at once. Barbara cut the controls so the Batwing dropped into a dive. The Bat Kayak bazooka zoomed through the sky, heading for a target that was no longer there. Instead of hitting the Batwing, the bazooka slammed into the zeppelin with a mighty explosion.

"Joker!" said the Riddler. "You blew up the zeppelin!"

"Hey, back off, man," the Joker said. "I'm going through a lot here."

19

O n the ground, the smoke lifted, revealing the wreckage of the Batwing. It had crash-landed on Wayne Island. The nosedive had been too deep and too fast to pull out of, but somehow everyone had survived.

"Woo! We did it!" Dick exclaimed.

"We did it, all right," Alfred added.

"Well done, everyone," Barbara congratulated them all.

"That was incredible! I feel so jazzed," said Batman.

"I say 'jazzed'!" Dick said.

"We were really firing on all cylinders there, huh?" said Batman.

"Nailed it!" cried Barbara.

"That was amazing," said Batman.

"I can't believe that worked!" Barbara said. "I gotta give it to you, Batman. That was awesome."

"And YOU were awesome!" Batman told Dick, Alfred, and Barbara. "And I was amazing. I'm not trying to make it about myself, obviously; I just want to make sure everyone gets a pat on the back ... because it feels good!"

"It does feel good!" said Dick.

"We had all these great ideas together. You had a good idea, and you had a good idea, and you had a good idea, and I had a good idea. You know what?" Batman pulled out his Good Idea Counter. "I think that collectively, I'm going to add—one."

The counter now stood at:

BATMAN: 5,678,483
EVERYONE ELSE: 1

"No way!" said Dick. "Let's all take a photo. All right, everyone, squeeze together." He pulled out the smartphone Batman had given him earlier.

"All right!" said Barbara.

"Splendid," said Alfred.

"I want to hold on to this moment forever, and commemorate it as the time we almost lost," said Dick.

"That's a great idea," Batman commented. "Commemorate."

Dick gathered everyone together and held his arm out as far as it would go. As they all smiled, Dick instructed, "Say family!"

"Family!" Alfred and Barbara and Batman chanted.

Dick snapped the shot and pulled in the phone to look at the group selfie. "Wow," he said. "My first family photo. Dad, didn't it turn out great!"

Dick handed Batman the phone, and then ran ahead with Barbara. "And now on to the next part of our dangerous mission! Bonds will be tested, alliances will be broken and reborn like a phoenix out of the fire . . ."

Batman took a long look at the family selfie. Then he swiped through some of the other pictures Dick had taken during their adventures. Batman smiled. The kid had captured some really epic moments.

Then he swiped to a picture of a picture—the one of him and his parents that hung in the Wayne Family gallery, the one that he sometimes talked to when he was lonely.

Alfred's words echoed in his head: *Your greatest fear is being part of a family again.*

"We might find some hidden treasure!" Dick exclaimed, interrupting Batman's reverie.

"Dick, I don't think there's any hidden treasure at Wayne Manor," Barbara said kindly.

Dick turned and ran back to Batman, his arms extended. Batman stopped him by holding on to his head. "Whoa. What are you doing?" he asked the kid.

"I'm trying to give you a big old hug," Dick replied.

"This is nice," said Barbara, smiling.

"I am so proud of you, sir," said Alfred.

"Okay, just back off a second," Batman said, trying to clear his head. "Give me a little space, guys, all right? It's just that this mission to infiltrate Joker Manor is going to be filled with all sorts of deadly foes . . ."

"We got this," said Barbara.

". . . and probably a bunch of clown-themed booby traps," Batman went on.

"Cool!" said Dick.

"So salvage what you can of the Batwing, and maybe root around and see if you can find us a couple of mineral waters, okay?" He paused and swallowed. "Then we'll head out."

"Yes, you got it, Dad Two," said Dick. He ran toward the Batwing. Alfred and Barbara followed him.

"I think I'll need snowshoes," Dick said as he began looking through the Batwing's glove compartment.

"I don't think you'll need snowshoes, but can you grab me that flashlight?" Barbara replied.

Batman watched as they all piled diligently into the cockpit. Then he stepped forward and closed the cockpit dome ... locking Alfred, Barbara, and Dick inside!

"Batman!" Barbara called.

"Sir!" Alfred called.

"Dad!" Dick called.

"What are you doing?" Barbara cried, banging on the shatterproof dome. "Hey, Batman! Please ... wait!"

Batman glanced at the three people in the cockpit. Then he turned away.

"Computer!" he called.

"Yes, sir?" replied Computer.

"I'm locking in some coordinates," Batman said. "Take the Batwing to the ice-cream shop on the border between Gotham City and Blüdhaven."

"No!!" cried Alfred, Barbara, and Dick.

"I want you to get these guys a couple of milk shakes and then keep them there till this whole thing blows over, okay?" Batman went on.

"Dad!" cried Dick.

"GO!"

"Batman, no!" cried Barbara.

"Go! Go!" Batman said.

"Batman, please, listen to me!" said Barbara. "Don't do this! You're doing the wrong thing!"

Batman closed his eyes and walked away from the team. Then he released a smoke bomb and disappeared.

Batman strode toward Wayne Manor. He straightened up, trying to figure out why he felt so bad. *Shake it off*, he told himself. *You're Batman.*

Fortunately, it was easy to sneak into Wayne Manor, which had become Joker Manor. All the rich, polished wood had been replaced with colored plastic and bright, fluorescent lights. It wasn't long before he found a clown-themed booby trap.

Batman watched warily as empty roller-coaster cars rolled past. Smiling faces had been painted on the car doors. Where the roller-coaster

track disappeared around a bend, there was a large, blinking neon sign. "Tunnel of Villainy," Batman read out loud. "Hilarious." He shook his head.

"You're going down, clown," he said. "Okay, let's get the projector and end this thing. Everybody ready?" Batman turned his head to check with his team, who wasn't there.

"What is the matter with me?!" he asked, slapping his own face. "Snap out of it, Bats! You're on your own, just like you're supposed to be."

Meanwhile, the Batwing was speeding toward the border between Gotham City and Blüdhaven. Barbara was pleading with Computer. "Please, Computer, you have to take us back," she said.

"I'm sorry," Computer replied. "I cannot override my system protocol."

"But, Computer, Batman's in danger," Barbara pointed out. "Aren't you programmed with Isaac Asimov's Three Laws of Robotics?"

"Yes."

"What are they?" Barbara asked.

"Something about obeying people and not hurting them," said Computer. "And also, I should

protect myself if I can. Seems like we're currently ticking all those boxes."

"Computer, Batman is not the same Batman he was. Can you please check in on him?" Alfred asked.

"All right," Computer agreed. "Accessing Batsuit diagnostics."

Back at Wayne Manor, Batman was using his grappling hook to rappel his way up to an open window. He slipped in the window and strode down the halls of his own home. It no longer resembled the place he knew and loved.

"Oh, hellooo, Batman..." came a familiar, unfriendly voice over the loudspeaker. "Gee, what happened to your friends?"

Batman whirled around, trying to figure out where the voice was coming from. He looked over his shoulder and saw the Joker standing there with his huge, unnatural grin.

"My friends?" Batman questioned. "The only friends I have are right here!" He held up his fists, boxing style. "Allow me to introduce you!" he barked, lunging forward.

But his fist didn't hit the Joker; it hit a funhouse mirror. "What?"

"Ha ha!" laughed the Joker. The shrill sound echoed through the tunnel. "That wasn't me. That was a man in the mirror! Woo-hoo! Ha ha ha. Look in the mirror, Batman," the Joker chided.

But what was staring at Batman was the Joker's reflection. Batman turned around and saw the Joker in every direction. He punched one. *SMASH.* And another. *SMASH.* He felt his rage rise as he tried to defeat the grinning villain. *SMASH, SMASH, SMASH.*

"Do you get the joke yet, Batman?" the Joker asked. "Everywhere you go, there I am!" The Joker cackled with glee. "I've always been right there with you."

Back in the Batwing, Computer was growing concerned. "Warning: Batman is not operating at mission optimum."

"See, Computer? He needs us!" Dick cried. "Please, take us back."

"But I must obey Batman's commands," Computer objected.

"No, by obeying him, you are allowing him to come to harm," Barbara argued. "Do you really want the man who made you to come to harm?"

The Batwing stopped. "You have just managed to fry my logic circuits and melt my heart," Computer announced. "System protocol—override. Let's go get him!"

With that, the Batwing turned around and headed back to Wayne Manor.

"Thanks, Computer!" Barbara said.

And just in the nick of time, too, because Batman was in trouble.

"Joker, I'm going to take that projector and send you back where you belong. And this time, I'm sending all your Rogue buddies with you."

"Sure, Batman," the Joker said sweetly. "You can have the projector. Just as soon as you tell me what I want to hear."

"What's that?" asked Batman wearily.

"Say that I'm your greatest enemy," the Joker replied. "That we belong together. That I *mean* something to you."

"Hold on . . . you mean all you want . . . is for me to say that you mean something to me?" Batman

said incredulously. "Then you'll give me the Phantom Zone Projector?"

"Yes!" said the Joker impatiently. "I thought I'd been crystal clear on that point!"

"Okay, sure, whatever," Batman said. "Joker-you-mean-something-to-me," he mumbled.

"I'm sorry, what was that? I couldn't hear what you said," the Joker replied, cocking his ear.

"I said: Joker-you-mean-something-to-me," Batman repeated.

"You said it too fast. Speak clearly," the Joker said.

"Ugh!" Batman said in exasperation. "Joker... you... mean... something... to... me..."

"Insincere!" the Joker cried. "Once more, with feeling."

"Look, I'm not an actor, all right? Just give me back the projector!" Batman said.

"Say it, Batman!" the Joker hollered.

"Look, I don't know what you want from me," said Batman. As he spoke, he Bataranged the image in front of him.

The mirror shattered. Behind it was a small battalion of drones, which reminded Batman of how Dick had defended the team so diligently. He remembered the great feeling he'd had working with Barbara and Alfred.

147

But the Joker's taunts soon brought him back to the Tunnel of Villainy.

Batman watched as the Joker's reflection bent over and reached down. When the villain stood back up, he was holding the Phantom Zone Projector.

"Unbelievable, Batman. You must really want to be alone. You abandoned your team, you blew off your friends, and you won't even say one thing to acknowledge the role I played in your life. I've had it. If you want to be alone so bad, I know a place where you can be alone forever."

The Joker hoisted the Phantom Zone Projector on his shoulder and took aim.

In a flash, Batman realized something. He didn't want to be alone.

Batman didn't even know if he could defeat the Joker on his own. He did, however, know just the people who could help him do it.

Before the Joker could make a move, Batman sprang into action. He spun around like a tornado, drop-kicking one drone after another. He booted them at the remaining mirrors. Then he turned and fled, leaving the Joker alone in the Tunnel of Villainy.

Batman headed right back in the direction he had come from—back to his team.

20

Meanwhile, the Batwing had landed outside Wayne Manor.

"Come on, everyone," Barbara urged Alfred and Dick. "We need to help Batman before he tries to do it all by himself."

But before Alfred, Barbara, and Dick could figure out the best way to infiltrate Wayne Manor, they were swarmed by Rogues.

"Oh dear . . . ," said Alfred.

By the time Batman emerged from Wayne Manor, things were not as he had left them. The Batwing was there, but his friends were not.

"Where's Dick?" Batman asked. "Where are

Alfred and Barbara?" The cockpit of the Batwing was empty. He stood next to the burning debris and rubbed his forehead.

"Computer," he said, lifting the comm link close to his mouth. "Show me the orphan I adopted."

"Yes, sir," Computer's voice came over the hand wrist device, and soon a holographic image of Dick appeared. The scene made Batman wince. The Rogues had captured Dick, and he was tied up. They appeared to be unloading him from a vehicle outside the Gotham City Energy Plant.

"That's no good," Batman murmured. "Now show me Barbara Gordon."

The hologram switched to an image of the new commissioner. She was back in her police clothes, chasing a band of Rogues.

"That's no good, either," Batman said. "She'll never defeat them that way. And she looked *way* better in her Batman merch outfit. What about Alfred?"

Batman was almost afraid to see what trouble his trusty butler had gotten into. But when the hologram flashed to a third projection, the old man appeared to be back inside Wayne Manor. Alfred had a sponge in his hand and was cleaning up the epic mess the Joker and his Rogues had left behind in the kitchen.

Batman considered his options. Maybe he should he let Alfred finish in the kitchen? It pained him to see what the Rogues had done to his sanctuary.

But Batman quickly came to his senses. He needed Alfred. He sent him a message to meet up by the entrance to the Batcave.

As dependable as always, Alfred showed up within moments. "You wanted me, sir?" the butler asked.

"How did you get out of the cockpit?" Batman asked.

"Ms. Gordon convinced Computer to turn the Batwing around," Alfred said. "She can be quite persuasive."

Batman shook his head. That new commissioner had a lot going for her.

"As soon as we were out, Master Dick insisted on fighting the Rogues on his own," Alfred explained. "His exact words were, 'my dad fights alone, and so do I!'"

"That's ridiculous," Batman said. He took a deep breath. "Alfred, we have to rescue Dick, and we need to save Gotham City. And we'll need Commissioner Gordon's help."

"You think she will help you?" Alfred asked, raising an eyebrow.

"We need to work together," Batman insisted. "Like when she flew the plane and you shot the bad guys and Dick swatted the drones and I told everyone what to do. We need to work like that. It's the only way."

Alfred nodded. "Like a team," he said.

"Yeah," Batman agreed. "Like that."

Moments later, they were MasterBuilding a Batcopter. Once they'd lifted off, they went into hot pursuit...of Commissioner Barbara Gordon.

"There she is, sir," Alfred announced, pointing at a grassy patch in the center of the city. "It looks like she's nearly cornered a Rogue."

"We cornered her first," Batman insisted, touching down—and allowing the Rogue to scamper off down a secluded street. "Hey, Barbara!" he called as he jumped out of the Batcopter.

"Seriously?" Barbara was annoyed. She looked Batman in the eye. "I almost had that guy!"

"That was just one Rogue. We can catch a lot more a lot faster, if we work together," Batman tried to explain.

"I don't believe this," the commissioner muttered.

"Wait, wait, okay, don't...," Batman stammered. He knew it was his fault that Dick had taken off again. He knew it was his fault that the new commissioner was angry, and that she didn't believe he was willing to work like a team. "Barbara, please. Don't leave."

Barbara turned back to look at him. "Why?"

"Because there's something I need to say to you."

"Go ahead," Barbara said, but she refused to look him in the eye.

Click.

"Click? Click doesn't mean anything, Batman," Barbara snapped.

"Sorry, you've got to turn around," Batman explained.

Barbara turned around to see the Bat-Signal blazing in the sky over Wayne Manor. But it wasn't the classic, old-fashioned Bat-Signal. This one was new and improved. It was wearing a red wig and bright pink lipstick.

"I call it the 'Babs-Signal,'" Batman explained. "And I'm flipping the switch ... for you. Because I need your help, Barbara. We need to save Dick and round up the Joker and his Rogues, and I can't do it alone. Do you think you can find any room in your Utility Belt for a narcissistic, self-centered, egotistical crybaby?"

Batman paused for a moment. "What do you say, Commissioner? Will you work with me?" He extended his hand hopefully.

Barbara held out for a while, and then she finally gave in and shook Batman's hand. "I thought you'd never ask," she said.

"Okay!" said Batman. "Team Gotham City Family is ready. Right, guys?"

"Right!" Alfred and Barbara cheered.

Ten minutes later, Alfred and Barbara had suited up in their deluxe Batman-themed gear again. The new team began to devise a plan.

As soon as the new, improved Bat-Signal started blazing in the sky, local police officers had started to gather.

"All right, team," Barbara announced. "I'm going to need to know everyone's abilities. And Batman, our team could really use some sweet Bat-gadgets."

"Absolutely," Batman answered, scanning the group of Gotham City's finest police officers. "I'm totally willing to share my stuff. This one time. But listen, if we're going to do that, Batman's

going to have to let you in on a little secret. Are you ready?"

"Okay," Barbara answered warily.

"All my weapons and tech are under Wayne Manor," he said. "Because I'm Bruce Wayne . . ."

Everyone in the crowd gasped.

". . .'s roommate," Batman finished. "I'm Bruce Wayne's roommate."

"Ohhhh," was the collective response.

"Oh, roommates," said one police officer. "That makes sense."

"As a single guy, it's a way to save money," agreed a motorcycle cop as he put on his helmet.

"Okay, well," Barbara said. "To the Batcave!"

"All right, guys, take whatever you need!" Batman instructed as they hurried into the Batcave. Then he took a good look around.

After the Joker and Batman's showdown in the Tunnel of Villainy, the Joker and his Rogues had cleared out of Wayne Manor, leaving much of Batman's stash of gear and weapons in a huge pile of rubble. There were bricks scattered everywhere.

"Uh, okay, no problem," Batman said. "I've been meaning to upgrade my fleet anyway. Everyone, grab some bricks! We're gonna make some new and improved Bat-vehicles!"

The police scattered and began building. Some ran to the vehicle bay, while others dove into the gadget cabinets. Everyone began building together.

"Oh yeah! Now, that's what I'm talking about!" Barbara said when Batman wheeled out trunks full of extra bricks. The entire crew got to work, enhancing the fleet of Bat-vehicles. Batman and his team didn't stop until each and every one had enlarged cockpits with ample seating. Now, they were all multihero vehicles!

The end result was beautiful. It was teamwork at its best.

"Yeah? Well, it gets better," Batman assured Barbara. "Wait for it!" He began to MasterBuild a Batwing just for the new commissioner.

"Whoo! That is amazing." Barbara's words were full of admiration, and Batman felt a sense of pride—a pride that wasn't confident or cocky. It was something that wasn't just about him. It was something good.

Everyone piled into the new rides. Batman and

Alfred settled into the Batmobile. Batman fired up the engine.

"Atomic batteries to power. Turbines to speed," said Computer.

"Okay! We have a bunch of Rogues to fight!" Barbara reminded the team. "So, if we're going to save the city, we need to combine our powers, look out for one another, and prove that teamwork makes the dream work. Are you guys ready?"

The troops were rallied! Everyone cheered.

"Let's do thi—"

But Batman interrupted her. "Wait-wait-wait! Hold on, one sec—" He jumped out of his vehicle and ran from car to car to train to boat to dune buggy. "Everybody, seat belts! Seat belt, seat belt, seat belt, seat belt, and . . . seat belt." He strapped in every last member of the Batman Team, and then hopped back in the Batmobile.

"Sir, your seat belt," reminded Alfred.

"Thanks, Alfred. Good to go!"

"Now let's do this!" Barbara cried.

21

The Gotham City Energy Plant was all lit up. It seemed to shine in the darkness of night.

Inside, the Rogues were feeling particularly proud of themselves. "Hahahahahahahaha," they laughed, giddy with their own badness.

"Sssshhhh. Quiet," Harley Quinn said. "What's that?"

A deep rumble seemed to be rising up from the ground.

"I think it's one of those traveling rave parties," Mr. Freeze said. He was fully recovered from his earlier battle with Batman and friends.

"Or it's an anthem for a team of scrappy under-dogs," suggested Kite Man.

"It's a team of scrappy underdogs!" Man-Bat screeched. "Destroy them!"

Rolling toward the plant, Batman's team was prepared for battle. The Bat-vehicles lined up, ready to take their best shot.

"Team Gotham City Family, activate!!!" Barbara yelled out. With all the vehicles aimed at the main power plant door, they delivered a massive blow.

"Sick work, Babs!" Batman said, assessing the damage with his night goggles. "We're almost in."

"Incoming!" someone called, and there was a mighty explosion on the heroes' side of the line.

"That was close! Everyone okay?" Barbara checked.

"Yeah!" responded the team.

"Great," Barbara said. It was time to come up with a proper plan. "The Joker will have the projector," she began. "So let's split up. My team will go after him. Your team should go find Dick," she said to Batman. "And Alfred will go after the rest of the Rogues."

"Ten-four, Commissioner Gordon," replied Batman.

The team cheered as they got ready to storm the plant.

"Okay, Alfred. Bring the pain!" directed Batman as Alfred punched keys on a control panel.

Alfred saluted as he commanded Computer to fire a final blast into the plant compound.

Alfred plowed straight ahead down the web of hallways and didn't stop until he had crashed the Batmobile into the core room, clearing the way for the rest of the Batman Team.

As soon as they reached the core room, Batman spotted Dick. The boy was tied up, hanging high in the air. Directly under him was a vat of lava with a mechanical shark swimming inside. And on the other side was the energy core. Piled on the core were countless explosives, big and small. They formed a giant pyramid, and they were all wired to one timer, which was quickly ticking down. It was very messy and extremely complicated.

The shark was nibbling at Dick's toes. "Get away from me, mean fish!" Dick cried.

"Get your jaws away from him, you big, bad shark!" Batman cried.

Dick pulled the can of Bat Shark Repellent out of his costume. "Dad, can we use this?"

Before Batman could answer, he'd sprayed the shark in the face. "It worked!"

That's when the Joker appeared from behind the pyramid. He looked especially happy to see Batman. After all, the Joker was on the brink of destroying everything that Batman held dear. Plus, he held the Phantom Zone Projector, so he had added ammunition.

The Joker lifted the Phantom Zone Projector and took a moment to survey the room through its viewfinder. His gaze came to rest on young Dick Grayson.

"Get away from him, you petty criminal!" said Batman. "Hold on, Robin! I'm coming for you!"

"Robin?" Dick said, realizing it was the first time Batman had called him that.

The rest of Batman's team had entered the core room, and they were piling out of their vehicles. They, too, had weapons raised. Their weapons were aimed at the Joker, and they were swarming in.

Seeing his chance, Batman wrapped a grappling hook around a high beam, retracted the cord, and shot straight up in order to cut Dick free. "I gotcha," Batman said. He grabbed his son and held him tight until they were both back on solid ground.

Once they had landed, Batman pulled Dick even closer. "You okay, buddy? Come here. You all right?"

"Yeah, yeah, I'm okay," Dick said, feeling the warmth of his dad's hand on his shoulder.

"Great, how you feeling?"

"Good," Dick responded, sensing his dad was hinting at something.

"You ready to do something cool?"

"Yeah! Always!" Dick confirmed.

"Great!" Batman responded, looking Dick in the eye. "You and me. Stay by my side."

Dick felt the excitement swell in his chest. This was really happening!

"We're about to do some super-hero-sidekick stuff," Batman explained. "It's just too bad you didn't bring your costu—"

RIP! With a quick tear, Dick revealed that he still had his costume on under his clothes.

"Incredible showmanship, kid," Batman said. "Okay, Robin. Together we're going to punch these guys so hard, words describing the impacts will spontaneously materialize in the air. And we're going to do it to the greatest fight song ever written. Now let's have some fun!"

On cue, a horn-heavy fight song began to blast over the Batmobile's speakers. The father-and-son duo began to blast the Rogue battalion. *POW! BAM! SMASH! KAPOW! WHAM! SPLAT!*

Together, they took out the bad guys. And they did it with smiles on their faces.

Meanwhile, Barbara Gordon was still circling above the plant. From the Batwing, she could see many of her police officers, members of the Batman team, staking out positions on the roof. She was waiting for her moment. Her instincts told

162

her that the Joker would attempt an escape from the chaos. She was sure that he'd appear through the roof hatch any minute now.

"All right, team," Barbara said when she saw the hatch open. "Let's shut them down!"

She hit the EJECT button and shot out of the plane, landing on the energy-plant roof. She found herself face-to-face with the Joker. He was holding the Phantom Zone Projector.

"Joker," Barbara said, "we have you surrounded."

But as soon as Barbara approached him, the Joker tossed the projector to Harley Quinn. When Barbara took a step toward Harley, she passed it to Catwoman.

The Rogues were like a bunch of football players passing the projector back and forth.

Barbara knew there wasn't time for a game of catch. There was a bomb *tick, tick, ticking* below. So she pulled out her ultradeluxe titanium grappling hook. When Catwoman set up for the next Rogue pass, Barbara threw her grappling hook like a lasso and reined in the Phantom Zone Projector. Interception!

But Barbara didn't have a chance to use the projector before Poison Ivy charged at her.

"Give it to me or I'll blow you a kiss," the toxic villain threatened.

"Into the core room," Barbara shouted to her teammates. "Follow me!"

Now it was the good guys' turn to play "pass the projector." As they descended the stairs to the ground floor of the energy plant, they threw the projector from one to another. Their moves were like basketball stars, with long reaches and spin fakes. One team member lobbed the projector up, and another leaped high to claim it.

"Get it back, you fools!" demanded the Joker as the group joined the messy battle on the Gotham City Energy Plant floor.

Batman and Dick were still doing double duty, fighting four Rogues together. Dick was attempting to wear down Croc by snaking under his legs and hitting him from behind while Batman pounded Croc and Bane alternately.

Alfred had joined in the projector hot potato.

"What about the bomb?" Barbara yelled to Batman.

"No time yet," Batman replied.

"I'll do it!" Dick volunteered, and he scampered up the pyramid of explosives before anyone could intervene. "I always fixed the Internet and cable at the orphanage," he called from the top of the mound of dynamite.

There wasn't a second to spare. The timer on

the detonator was at 00:59. Dick knelt down and investigated the wires, which didn't look nearly as bad as the administrators' phone-charging station.

The Joker wanted the projector back, and he wanted it back NOW! He tossed insults at the Rogues every time the Bat Team tossed the projector.

"Alfred, catch!" Barbara yelled as the device whizzed through the air.

Alfred got nervous when Kite Man swooped down toward him. "Batman!" he yelled, hurtling the projector at the Caped Crusader.

Batman dodged a power-packed punch from Bane to snatch the projector.

The Joker charged him. "That's mine," the Joker declared.

"Uh, no," Batman replied. "Technically, this belongs to Superman." He turned to Barbara, and then stepped aside so she could take his place before the Joker. "And technically, *you* belong in Arkham Asylum."

Barbara pulled a pair of handcuffs out of her Utility Belt. "Joker, you have the right to remain silent . . ." she began, cuffing the Joker.

Batman winked at the Joker. "Gotcha," he said.

"I got it!" Dick called out from the top of the bomb tower. "And there were still two seconds left! No pressure at all." He raised his arms in victory and then slid down the pile of explosives.

Alfred, Barbara, Batman, and Dick hugged and shared high fives with the other members of the Bat Team. They'd done it!

Barbara and the police force began rounding up the Rogues. Within moments, they were lined up behind the Joker, ready for their return trip to Arkham Asylum.

Batman looked at the Phantom Zone Projector in his hands and smiled ruefully. He knew what he had to do.

He tucked the projector under his arm and crossed to the other side of the room.

"Dad, where're you going?" Dick called after him.

"I have to return this," Batman tried to explain. "To Superman."

"Then I'll go with you," Dick insisted, looking up at his dad's chiseled face. "Just like old times."

"I'm sorry, son," Batman replied, putting his hand on Dick's shoulder. "I have to do this alone."

"Dad Two! Please!" Dick begged.

"Call me—" Batman paused and removed his mask. "Dads."

Dick was excited and confused. "My two dads are the same dad!!!!" he cried. "But they're both leaving." The realization nearly crushed him.

Batman could see how scared Dick was at the thought of losing him again. He leaned down and looked his son in the eye. "It's going to be okay, kid," Batman promised. "Sometimes people need some time alone. Sometimes they need to do something on their own. But that doesn't mean that they don't need other people, too. Some very wise people taught me that." He glanced up at Alfred and Barbara and smiled.

Dick took those words in and held them close. Then he looked up at his dad one last time . . . and hugged him as hard as he could.

Batman hugged him back. "You know what our superpower is? It's our family."

He picked up the projector. "Good luck, Barbara. I know you'll be the commissioner Gotham City needs."

Barbara smiled wistfully. "Thanks, Batman. I'll work with the whole department to look after Gotham City while you're gone."

"So long, Alfred," Batman said. "I'll see you soon."

Batman nodded at the man who had cared for Bruce Wayne and Batman for so many years. Then he took off for the Fortress of Solitude.

22

A short while later, in the Wayne Manor kitchen . . .

"What are we all looking at?" Batman asked.

"Dad!" cried Dick.

"Crime-fighting partner!" cried Barbara.

"Son!" cried Alfred.

Alfred, Barbara, and Dick all beamed at Batman.

"Reverse smoke bomb!" Batman said jokingly, because, instead of disappearing after a smoke bomb, he had mysteriously appeared. "Ha ha ha ha," he chuckled. "I kind of love surprising you guys. It's become my thing."

"Welcome home!" the members of his Batman family greeted him.

"That didn't take long at all," Dick said with relief.

"Well, yeah. Superman wasn't feeling all that chatty," Batman admitted.

He stood there for a moment, taking it all in. Who knew that opening up your home—and your heart—to other people could make you feel safer, more complete?

"What are we going to do now, Barbara?" he asked.

"Rebuild the city, I guess," she answered.

"Together," stated Batman. "That's a great idea."

"But first, how about we eat?" Alfred suggested. "I've prepared a complete menu for us all. The main course is Lobster Thermidor."

"My favorite," said Batman.

"This is great, guys," Dick said, looking around the table. "I've always wanted to have a family dinner."

"It sure is, Dick," Barbara agreed.

"You know what they say, Master Dick," Alfred added. "'The family that dines together, fights crime together.' Am I right?"

"You're right, Alfred. Cheers." Batman raised his glass. He raised it to that moment and all the other small moments that make up family life. He raised

it to the photo of his new family he would add to the Wayne Family Gallery. He raised it to dinner at the table and movie nights in the den. And then he raised his glass a little higher, this time, to having three smart, skilled, and brave teammates to help in the constant battle to keep Gotham City safe.

Cheers!